A Harlequin Romance

OTHER

Harlequin Romances

by LUCY GILLEN

Many of these titles are available at your local bookseller,
or through the Harlequin Reader Service.

For a free catalogue listing all available Harlequin Romances,
send your name and address to:

HARLEQUIN READER SERVICE,
M.P.O. Box 707, Niagara Falls, N.Y. 14302
Canadian address: Stratford, Ontario, Canada N5A 6W4

or use order coupon at back of books.

THE HUNGRY TIDE

by

LUCY GILLEN

Harlequin Books

TORONTO • LONDON • NEW YORK • AMSTERDAM • SYDNEY • WINNIPEG

Original hardcover edition published in 1975
by Mills & Boon Limited

ISBN 0-373-01995-5

Harlequin edition published August, 1976

CHAPTER ONE

RACHEL paid the taxi driver, then stood and watched the taxi out of sight down the long winding drive before she turned back to look at the house again. Seaways was impressive by any standards, a typical monument to Victorian solidity but hardly welcoming. It had a secret, closed look that was somehow discouraging, especially to someone like Rachel who was not at all certain that she should not have gone round to a servants' entrance, if there was one.

Hastily dismissing a moment of panic, she mentally shook herself and went up the three steps to a massive door made from dark timber planks studded over with black iron bolts. Huge bay windows reflected the darkness of a winter's day and faced on to a garden that consisted mostly of rather tired-looking shrubs as far as Rachel could see, although it must have been quite pretty in spring and summer when the rhododendrons were in flower and the willowy bareness of the forsythia was clothed in yellow and pale green.

A hesitant pull on the bell knob brought an almost immediate response in the person of a middle-aged woman with greying hair who smiled and indicated that she should come inside. The way the woman nodded her head seemed to indicate that she recognised her name, and for that small relief Rachel thanked heaven.

'Will you come with me?' the woman said, and led the way across a hall that in no way matched the Victorian appearance of the outside of the house.

It was light and airy and there was no sign of the dark walls and furniture Rachel had expected to see in such a house. Deep red carpet deadened their footsteps and the gloomy grey daylight admitted by one of the smaller windows showed everything to be white and gold.

Even the ornately carved staircase was white-painted and its intricate balustrades gilded. Several watercolours displayed their misty pastels against white walls and a delightful Capo di Monte figure of an old man had pride of place on a small spindle-legged table against one wall.

The woman, presumably a housekeeper, opened a door to one side of the hall and stepped just inside to announce her arrival, almost as if she was a visitor instead of a prospective employee. 'Miss Carson's here, sir,' she told the occupant of the room, then stood aside to let Rachel in, smiling encouragement as she closed the door behind her.

The room she found herself in surprised Rachel less than it might have done if she had not already seen the hall outside, for the same taste was reflected in the decor here. It was a big room with an open fire burning in the wide fireplace, but it was evident from the warmth that the fire served merely as a boost to a central heating system that was not at once evident.

Here too the furniture was light and elegant and in perfect taste, more Georgian than Victorian in period and obviously none of it copied. Whatever else Mr. Neil Brett's property betrayed about him it stressed that he was not a poor man or he could not have indulged such tastes.

The man himself when he turned towards her was almost as much of a surprise as the interior of his house had been, and Rachel wondered if she had ever seen a man so definitely blond before. He was tall, over six feet, she guessed, and rakishly lean with hair that was thick and pale as corn-silk and light blue eyes that regarded her steadily as she hesitated to come across the room.

She thought he looked rather surprised, as if something about her was not exactly what he expected, but her own reaction to him startled her most of all. His presence seemed to fill the big room and the force of his personality was such that it was almost overpowering.

He did not come forward to meet her, but waited instead for her to join him by the massive grey marble mantel, saying nothing but conveying his wishes by merely standing there and looking across at her. Her own rather petite stature made long steps impossible and it seemed to take her an interminable time to cross the big room, while all the time he studied her with a frank appraisal that was embarrassing in its intensity.

Her long dark hair curled softly about a small oval face and complemented huge grey eyes and a

7

mouth that trembled rather nervously at the moment, but she doubted if an appreciation of her looks was the reason for that steady scrutiny. Mr. Neil Brett would not be so easily impressed.

'Miss Carson?' He inclined his head but did not offer to shake her hand. With a similar gesture he indicated a chair immediately behind her, but remained standing himself, putting his hands behind his back and drawing back his shoulders. 'Please sit down!'

It was a command rather than an invitation, and Rachel obeyed it automatically. She could not have said just why she had expected him to be dressed in a formal suit and a tie and looking like a typical business man, but she could not have been more wrong. He looked rather more like a farmer than a business man and he had obviously made no special effort to appear formal for the interview.

Serviceable denims were tucked into short brown boots and revealed long muscular legs whose length was emphasised by the stance of his booted feet—set slightly apart and planted firmly on the dark green carpet. The sleeves of a faded brown denim shirt were rolled up above the elbows and showed strong brown arms and a column of tanned neck and throat with broad shoulders pulling the shirt tight across the front as he drew back his arms.

A dark golden tan was in such contrast to his blondness that Rachel found herself wondering what ancestry could have produced such colouring. It was particularly noticeable in the strong rugged face where the brown skin was quite startling

8

when it contrasted with such light blue eyes. He suggested power and a certain ruthlessness that was oddly disturbing, and Rachel's flesh tingled warningly.

'You're a trained children's nurse?' he asked, and she nodded, hastily bringing herself back to earth again.

'Yes, Mr. Brett,' she said. 'I qualified this year.'

'I see!'

Again she was subjected to that steady scrutiny and found it equally disturbing. He moved suddenly, a swift movement that at first startled her, and stood with both hands in his pockets, his shoulders resting against the tall mantel behind him. It was probably as near as he ever came to relaxing, Rachel thought, and again experienced that urgent warning tingle when she briefly met his eyes.

'You're younger than I would have expected,' he said bluntly. 'I presume you have the necessary certificates to prove your qualifications?'

'Naturally!' Colour warmed her cheeks, although the request was reasonable enough in the circumstances. No one, least of all a man as thorough as Neil Brett suggested, would be prepared to hand over the care of his child to just anyone who applied. She opened her handbag. 'I have them here if you want to see them,' she told him, and passed him the envelope containing her certificates.

He nodded his thanks and scrutinised the papers carefully before handing them back to her. 'I see that you qualified only two months ago,' he observed. 'Is this the first post you've applied for?'

The interview was not going quite as Rachel had imagined it and she felt dismayingly uneasy in this man's presence, more uneasy than she would have believed possible. 'I've been interviewed for one other place,' she admitted, wondering just how honest she could afford to be.

A raised brow made it obvious that she would have to be more specific than that. 'And?' he prompted shortly, and Rachel flushed, lifting her chin in an unconscious gesture of defiance.

'I was unsuitable for the job,' she told him, and saw the light blue eyes narrow swiftly when she made the admission.

'In what way unsuitable, Miss Carson?'

Rachel hesitated before she answered. It would be difficult trying to explain that the busy blonde society hostess who had interviewed her last had taken no more than five seconds to decide that Rachel was not what she was looking for at all. 'I wasn't given any specific reason,' she admitted. 'I was simply told that I wasn't right for the post, that's all.'

'Hmm!' One brow flicked upwards again and the blue eyes slid in swift appraisal over her small neat figure and the flushed prettiness of her face. 'Was the objection to your youth or your prettiness?' he asked, and Rachel's cheeks burned with embarrassment at his frankness.

'I—I wasn't told,' she insisted a little huskily. 'I was just told that I wasn't suitable and sent away.'

'Hmm!' Once again he made that short, non-committal comment and regarded her with a steady, disconcerting gaze for several seconds. 'In short, you've had no practical experience at all?' he observed, and Rachel frowned, wondering what he considered working with a dozen small children to be, if not practical.

'I've had quite a bit of practical experience,' she told him. 'Part of my training consisted of working in a children's home.'

One arched brow doubted the practicality of that in regard to the post he had in mind and his mouth curved derisively. 'This isn't a children's home,' he reminded her quietly. 'Have you had experience in private work—as a nurse to a child in a private home?'

Rachel, reluctantly honest, shook her head. 'Not yet, Mr. Brett.' She looked up at him briefly, irritated by the hopelessness of gaining the experience he set such score by if she could not first find someone willing to employ her. 'And it's difficult to see how I'm going to gain experience without being employed first!' she added with a hint of challenge.

'So you think I should pay you to gain experience?'

Rachel looked away again hastily, unable to quite hold that steady blue gaze with as much bravado as she would like. 'I *am* qualified,' she reminded him. 'You wouldn't be paying me for nothing, or for anything I'm not perfectly capable of doing! It's really not much of a gamble!'

Neil Brett stiffened, she was aware of it from the

corner of her eye, and her hands curled anxiously in her lap while she waited for his objection to her argument. 'Are you also trained to be impudent to your employer?' he asked coldly. 'Or is that part of your natural character, Miss Carson?'

Rachel hesitated. A natural pertness urged her to answer him with a retort that she was not prepared to suppress her own opinions completely, but she had a feeling that a lot depended on her answer. Perhaps even the fact of whether or not she got the post, and she was strangely anxious to have this job. Not simply because she had not yet found anything to suit her since she qualified, but because something about Neil Brett held a curious fascination for her and she wanted to work for him.

'I'm sorry if you think I was impudent,' she said, deceptively humble in her apology, 'but I *am* good at my job, Mr. Brett, and I want to gain experience—working for someone like you is the only way I can do that.'

He regarded her steadily for a moment longer, than nodded his head as if he had suddenly made up his mind about it. 'Very well, I'll give you a month's trial,' he decided shortly.

'Thank you!' It was strange the sense of relief she felt when he said that, and she wondered why on earth she should be so anxious to work for him when their first encounter had scarcely been encouraging.

'Are you accustomed to small boys?' he asked, and Rachel nodded, hardly daring to speak in case she said the wrong thing and he changed his mind again.

'I'm quite used to them,' she told him a little breathlessly. 'I was in charge of six or seven at a time during my training.'

He considered for a moment longer, his dark face shadowed and etched with the flickering light of the fire in the darkening room. Standing now with one arm along the marble mantel he looked down at the licking flames and Rachel thought he was far away mentally, if not physically.

One leg was bent, the foot resting on the wrought iron Victorian fender that guarded the fire, and she found it hard not to notice the tautness of fawn denim against the muscular curve of his leg. Neil Brett was a disturbing man and she would perhaps regret having tried so hard to work for him, but she found the prospect irresistible at the moment.

'Nicholas is four years old,' he told her suddenly, and brought her swiftly back to reality. 'He's quite a well behaved child, but you might have a little trouble managing him at first.'

He sounded, Rachel thought a little dizzily, as if he was talking about an animal rather than his own small son, and her sympathies were already with the child, Nicholas, however much of a problem he might prove to be.

She smiled in a way that left him in no doubt that she was perfectly capable of dealing with any tantrums the child might produce, whoever he was. 'One small boy isn't *so* difficult to cope with, Mr.

Brett,' she observed, perhaps with rather more contempt for his opinion than she realised, for Neil Brett was frowning again, his ice-blue eyes looking at her coolly.

'Your assurance will have more authority when you've met Nicholas and know him,' he told her firmly. 'Until then allow me to know best, Miss Carson!'

Rachel swallowed hard, trying to stem the retort that sprang to her lips. Then she inclined her head briefly and bowed to the inevitable—even on such short acquaintance it was easy to recognise that very few people would come unscathed from an encounter with Neil Brett. 'Yes, of course,' she said quietly. 'Am I to see Nicholas now?'

'No!'

The reply was prompt and adamant and Rachel frowned over it. One of the things her training had impressed upon her was the need for a certain rapport with her young charge, and a meeting before being committed to taking the post was preferable if not absolutely essential.

Rachel hesitated, uncertain how to proceed. With some employers it would probably have been possible to insist, or at least to stress the importance of that first meeting; but in the case of Neil Brett she doubted if any amount of insistence would do any good.

Because she had no intention of letting her dislike of the situation go unremarked, however, she sighed deeply in resignation and shook her head. 'Very well, Mr. Brett,' she said, 'but it is *quite* important that the right relationship is established as soon as possible. It's most important that your son likes me and that we get on well together—a preliminary meeting can establish from the outset whether or not we suit one another.'

Her reasons were of no interest to him at all, she realised, but there was a bright glitter in his light blue eyes as he stood there looking down at her steadily. 'My son?' he asked quietly, almost gently, and Rachel felt the colour flood into her cheeks when she realised the awful gaffe she had made.

Too stunned to speak for a moment, she shook her head slowly, not daring to look at him, her cheeks flaming as she sought for explanations, although heaven knew there were grounds enough for her assumption that the child was his son.

'I—I'm sorry, Mr. Brett,' she said, after several awful seconds, 'but I thought——'

'I suppose it was a natural assumption,' Neil Brett allowed coolly, without giving her time to finish her explanation. 'Nicholas is my nephew, Miss Carson, he is also my legal ward—do you know what that means?'

'Of course!' She flushed when she detected a hint of patronage in his voice. 'I assume that the little boy has no parents and the courts have appointed you his guardian.'

'More or less,' he allowed. 'Nicky's mother was my sister—there is no one else sufficiently interested in him to give him a home, so he's with me.' The light blue eyes looked at her from between thick brown lashes and a hint of what could have been a smile just touched the corners of his wide mouth. 'I may not be your conception of the perfect father, Miss Carson, but I'm all he has and so far he's made no complaint!'

'Oh no, I'm sure he hasn't!' She hastened to assure him on that point, for without doubt whatever other failings Neil Brett might have it was plain, to Rachel at least, that he was genuinely fond of his nephew.

He moved away from the fireplace suddenly, a swift restless movement that took him just out of Rachel's sight, and she wondered if she dared turn round in her chair to look at him. There was something about the man that she found irresistibly fascinating, despite the fact that he had scarcely gone out of his way to be charming.

He strode across to the window and stood for a moment there with his hands behind his back, his blond head held high on that strong brown column of neck. 'You need only know that Nicky's mother died last year,' he told her in a cool, flat voice that obviously disguised some deep emotion he refused to display. 'She was drowned in the sea only a mile from here.'

'Oh, I'm sorry!'

Her sympathy seemed to surprise him, for he turned round againd suddenly and faced her, his eyes carefully concealed by half-lowered lids, his face shadowed because his back was to the grey daylight outside the window behind him.

'I've told you this only because you must understand the need to handle Nicholas with care,' he told her quietly. 'He has what might appear to be an unreasonable fear of the sea, and I have forbidden anyone to take him near it until he's recovered from his fear.'

By anyone Rachel could only assume that he referred to the housekeeper and perhaps other servants who were given charge of the little boy until a nanny could be found for him. Her heart went out to Nicholas in his loneliness, for she felt sure that a small boy in a house full of grown-ups and consigned to the care of servants must be an incredibly lonely child.

'It's something he can be coaxed out of in time,' she said gently, and was startled when he immediately strode forward and stood over her, his light eyes glittering bright below drawn brows.

'He will be allowed to grow out of it in his own time, Miss Carson!' he told her forcefully. 'You will not attempt to work miracles, no matter what your training has led you to believe you're capable of! Do you understand?'

He stood close enough for her to be disturbingly aware of him in a way she had never experienced before. There was a stunning aura of maleness about him, of sheer masculine vigour that seared her senses like fire and left her breathless with its unexpectedness. Neil Brett was not a man to be taken lightly and she would have to learn to control her reactions if she was to work for him.

Warily she ventured an upward glance at him and saw that a fierce frown drew his fair brows together above the glitter of light blue eyes. In anger he was not only impressive but frankly overawing, and she nodded automatically.

'Yes, of course I understand, Mr. Brett,' she said as coolly as she was able, 'but I——'

'I sincerely hope you aren't one of those women who think they know everything there is to know about children, Miss Carson,' he declared forcefully. 'Are you?'

Rachel flushed indignantly, but her heart was racing, triggered by some inexplicable chemistry he aroused in her, and she found it difficult to answer him as calmly and matter-of-factly as she would normally have done. 'I've been trained to deal with almost every aspect of children, Mr. Brett,' Rachel told him, and tried hard to steady a voice that quivered dismayingly and gave quite the wrong impression. 'Of course, I don't claim to know everything about children, but I *do* know my job and——'

She almost gasped aloud when a harsh snort of impatience cut her explanation short. He dismissed her claim with a broad, contemptuous sweep of one large hand and it so suggested an impending blow that Rachel instinctively leaned backwards away from it, her head jerked up, holding the gaze of those glittering blue eyes for several seconds before she blinked in realisation.

'Do you wish to work for me or not, Miss Carson?' he demanded. His voice was quiet, but hinted at menace so that Rachel gazed at him anxiously while she tried to nod agreement.

'Yes, yes, of course I do,' she insisted, and at the

same time wondered if she had completely taken leave of her senses in wanting to work for such a man.

'Then you won't try making rule-book experiments at Nicky's expense!' he told her harshly. 'Is that quite clear?'

'Quite clear, Mr. Brett!' Rachel hastily ran her tongue over her lips before chancing another upward glance at that stern implacable face. 'I—you have quite the wrong impression of my intent,' she ventured. 'I wouldn't attempt anything without your consent, of course, and——'

'Good! Then there'll be no problems!'

Rachel stared at him, unsure which caused her most disturbance—his violent insistence on being obeyed implicitly, or the prospect of being in daily contact with a man who promised to to be much more of a problem than any employer she had envisaged during her training years.

There was simply no reason that she could see why she did not simply get up and walk out of the house here and now, leaving Mr. Neil Brett to deal with his own problems as best he could. But she was still influenced by that strange desire to stay and work for him and instead of walking out she waited.

For a moment Neil Brett stood looking down at her as she sat with her hands clasped over the handle of her bag, her cheeks flushed with the urgency of her heartbeat. It was quite ridiculous to allow a stranger to have such an effect on her and she was unsure whether she relished the idea or not of being so emotionally assaulted.

After a moment or two he moved away, going over to stand beside the mantel again, and she was uneasily aware that he was watching her. The flickering flames of the fire cast deep shadows on his strong tanned features, lending them even more character. An arrogant and disturbing man—too forceful to make him easy to work for, but too irresistible to simply walk away from.

The immediate necessity of finding someone to care for little Nicholas Browlett meant that Rachel was expected to take up her duties right away, and Neil Brett had straight away sent one of his staff with her to fetch her luggage. Her own plans and desires did not enter into it, apparently, for she was not consulted as to whether or not it was convenient for her to move in at once—it was taken for granted.

Despite the autocratic way she was enrolled into the household, however, she had no complaints about her accommodation, nor about the way she was teated. Mrs. Handley, the housekeeper, was delegated to supervise her moving in and she was allocated a room at the front of the house that was far better than anything she had expected.

It was large and airy and, despite the old-fashioned windows, admitted quite a lot of the grey winter light from outside. The furnishings again reflected Neil Brett's impeccable taste, so that she was always to be conscious of the man even in the privacy of her own room. No matter how brusque and earthily masculine he might be in person, it was evident that he had a collector's taste for fine things and furnished his house with them rather than locked them away for his own pleasure only.

The two windows gave her a magnificent view over rolling Kentish farmland, and beyond it, in the distance, a tell-tale luminosity in the sky betrayed the nearness of the sea. The sea that she was forbidden to visit with her little charge because his mother had been drowned in it.

She stood for a while at one of the windows looking out over the ploughed fields at the curlews and seagulls who gleaned a harvest of their own from the curling brown furrows, and wondered just how Nicholas' mother had died and why. Mrs. Handley probably knew, but she was not yet long enough established in the household to ask questions about the family.

'It's a wonderful view,' she said, and turned and smiled at the housekeeper.

Mrs. Handley's pleasant face responded with a smile. 'It's nicely placed,' she agreed in her quiet country voice. 'You'll like it here, I'm sure.'

Rachel opened a suitcase and began to take out some of her things while Mrs. Handley smoothed out invisible creases in the smooth perfection of a Victorian patchwork quilt. A whole string of questions were pressing for answers and unless she was mistaken the housekeeper was still with her for a reason. She could have left minutes ago, but she had not, instead she stood by the old-fashioned double bed and, without saying anything, gave the impression that she had something to say.

'I'm anxious to meet Nicholas,' Rachel told her, laying a dress carefully across the foot of the bed as she spoke. 'You know him quite well, of course, Mrs. Handley?'

'Ever since he was born, you might say,' the housekeeper agreed, and shook her head sadly.

'He's an orphan, I gather,' Rachel guessed, having heard nothing about Nicholas' father, and Mrs. Handley neither confirmed nor denied it.

'Poor little love,' she sympathised. 'It seems like everything's been against him, right from the beginning. Mind you,' she added hastily as if to rectify a wrong impression, 'he's happy enough here with his uncle, and he'll be better still now there's someone to care for him full time.'

It was a delicate position to be in and Rachel trembled at the prospect of saying the wrong thing, but she was near to the reason for Neil Brett's guardianship of his nephew, and to ask just one question was irresistible.

'I know about his mother being drowned last year,' she said, and saw the immediate change that came over Mrs. Handley's friendly face.

'Sad,' was all she said, and shook her head.

'And presumably he doesn't have a father, since Mr. Brett is his guardian,' Rachel ventured, only partially discouraged.

Mrs. Handley tightened her mouth and her round face took on a curiously closed look as she gave one last smoothing pat to the patchwork bedspread before walking towards the door. Turning in the doorway, she looked back at Rachel with a smile that was belied by the strange glittery look in her eyes. 'If there's anything more you need, Miss Carson,' she told her, 'just ask—either Betty or me will get it for you.'

Rachel blinked at her for a minute, taking time to grasp the fact that her attempt to probe into her charge's family affairs had been firmly and adamantly rebuffed. Whether Nicholas's father was alive or dead was obviously a matter Mrs. Handley refused to discuss.

'Thank you, Mrs. Handley,' she said after a moment, and the housekeeper closed the door quietly behind her.

CHAPTER TWO

Nicholas Browlett proved to be an easy child to get to know, and he had a charmingly old-fashioned manner that made one think he was older than in fact he was. Despite his uncle's warning that he might be difficult to handle initially, he seemed quite well adjusted and quite different from the nervous and unhappy child that Rachel had expected.

He was rather small for his four and a half years, but he looked robust enough, even though he was lacking the same healthy tan that made his uncle's looks so striking. There was little family resemblance, in fact, apart from their blue eyes, and Nicholas was altogether more typically English with his brown hair, round face and fair skin.

After two weeks they were beginning to get to know one another quite well and it was evident they were going to get along well. On the whole Rachel found him obedient and quite amenable, although he had showed swift resentment when she tried to make him refer to his uncle by his title instead of simply calling him Neil. He could be stubborn, Rachel thought ruefully, and would probably grow up to be as autocratic as Neil Brett if he was to spend the rest of his formative years in his charge.

Nicholas now sat on the long box seat that ran the whole width of the big bay window in the sitting-room, his feet curled up under him and a book that had failed to interest him abandoned beside him while he gazed out of the window. 'Don't you like your book?' Rachel asked, and he looked at her for a moment with a hint of impatience in his eyes.

'I don't like books,' he told her frankly, and she frowned.

'Oh, but you should enjoy them, Nicky,' she said. 'Shall I read that one to you? Would you like that?'

Nicky's head shook decidedly and he again looked out of the window. 'No, thank you,' he said firmly but politely. 'When Lars comes I can go riding every day.'

'Lars?' Rachel looked at him curiously. She had heard nothing about an expected visitor, but apparently whoever was coming was popular with Nicky, for his blue eyes glowed with the pleasure of anticipation.

'You don't know Lars,' he informed her, rather superfluously.

'No, I don't.' Rachel refused to question him about the identity of Lars, whoever it might be. The name sounded odd to her ears, but Nicky was probably not pronouncing it properly.

'Don't you want to know about him?' Nicky asked after a few seconds of meaningful silence, and Rachel could not restrain a smile.

It was obvious that he laid great store by the expected visitor, and he was only waiting to be asked before he launched into a spate of information about him. She ruffled his thatch of brown hair with her fingers and laughed softly. 'All right,' she conceded, 'you tell me about Lars—I presume he has another name too?'

Nicky was nodding his head eagerly. 'Lars Bergen,' he informed her with meticulous clarity. 'He's my—my sort of cousin.'

'Your cousin? Oh, I see!'

Rachel made a rapid mental adjustment to her picture of Lars Bergen, although she really had no idea why she had automatically assumed that the eagerly awaited visitor was a grown man and not another little boy, except that Nicky's world seemed bounded by grown-ups.

Of course he would look forward to the arrival of another child, although it raised the question in Rachel's mind whether she would be expected to take charge of both children while Lars Bergen was visiting.

The name of the visitor also made it fairly plain that the cousin was almost certainly of Scandinavian origin, and she thought that at last she saw a possible explanation for Neil Brett's blond looks.

'Can we go for a walk?' Nicky asked, and Rachel hastily blinked herself back to earth, nodding her head in agreement.

'Yes, of course we can,' she said, 'if that's what you'd like to do.'

She was nothing loath to go walking herself, for she was fond of the exercise and it would do Nicky good to have a spell in the fresh air. It was not even necessary to leave the grounds to enjoy quite a long walk, for they extended to several acres, apart from one or two farms and cottages that belonged to the estate.

So much she had learned from Mrs. Handley, who was willing enough to talk about the estate, though far less forthcoming about the family who owned it. It seemed to Rachel pretty certain that there was some kind of mystery somewhere in the family background, and she suspected it concerned her charge. Mrs. Handley did not seem a naturally secretive woman, but whenever the question of Nicky's parents arose she immediately became uncommunicative and changed the subject. Perhaps when she had been there a little longer—but that remained to be seen.

Rachel wrapped Nicky up well in a coat and scarf and insisted he wore gloves against the cold east wind that blew in off the not too distant sea, then she put on boots and a short thick jacket herself before they set off. A walk as far as the spinney at the bottom of the extensive gardens would give them both an appetite for lunch.

Tall, wide-spreading oaks sheltered the house from the worst of the winds and formed a protective screen between it and the rest of the estate. On an earlier walk Rachel had been delighted to discover that primroses and violets grew along the banks that bordered the ditches, although they were little more than clumps of bedraggled leaves at the moment, huddling below the bare arms of hazel and blackthorn.

Beyond the trees and hedges, the other side of the ditch, was rolling farmland enclosing a tall grey farmhouse in its midst and tall, conical coasthouses that stood like sentinels against the grey sky, awaiting the next September harvest of hops.

A few beef cattle scavenged for the last of the grass, eked out by substitute fodder from the yards, and it all looked so dismal at this time of year. But Rachel could imagine it much different in summer when the fields were lush and green and the now barren hop gardens were strung with their green vines. A warm, contented countryside that changed little and somehow offered the kind of peace it was difficult to find elsewhere.

Without quite realising she was doing it, Rachel smiled to herself, and Nicky, running back to join her, looked up at her curiously. 'Do you like it here, Miss Carson?' he asked, and Rachel nodded.

'I always liked Kent, Nicky,' she told him. 'I used to spend holidays here when I was a little girl.'

'Here?' Taking her literally, he looked puzzled, and she shook her head.

'Not actually here, at Seaways,' she explained. 'But not too far from here—by the seaside.'

She had for the moment genuinely forgotten about his aversion to the sea and the reason for it, for she would never have mentioned it if she had stopped to consider. It was a sudden strange look of withdrawal on his face that reminded her, and the droop of his mouth made her wish she had been more careful.

'I don't like the sea,' he told her in a flat little voice that touched a chord in her heart and made her want to drop down beside him and hug him close.

Instead she put a hand on his head and ran her fingers gently through the thick and slightly curly hair on top of his head. 'I know, Nicky,' she said quietly, 'and I'm sorry I mentioned it.'

'It doesn't matter.' He sounded so resigned and so adult that the effect was to tug even harder at her emotions.

His huge blue eyes looked up at her for a moment, and she would have reached down and cuddled him, but he was off suddenly across the muddy grass, making sounds that were presumably meant to represent an aeroplane, since his arms were spread wide and he dipped and turned as he ran, his cheeks bright with exertion and the keen coldness of the wind.

He played like that for some time, always just out of reach, so that Rachel began to wonder if he was doing it deliberately, and his course took them more towards the front of the house instead of the back as Rachel had intended. Then suddenly he turned and looked across to where, in the distance, the driveway up to the house wound between its secretive guard of oak trees.

'Lars is coming!' he cried in a shrill excited voice, and dashed off across the parkland before Rachel could do anything to stop him.

'Nicky!' She followed as quickly as she could, but she could not quite match his helter-skelter speed because she was much more wary of slipping and falling on the muddy grass. 'Nicky, wait!'

Nicky paid her no need but ran on, his little legs easily covering the ground, his arms pumping energetically at his sides as he ran, heedless of anything but getting to the visitor as quickly as possible, and Rachel, panting for breath, saw a long silver grey car sweep past the trees on the drive and felt her heart lurch wildly in fear.

If he got to the drive before she did herself he might so easily run straight out into the car, for he was such a small figure for a driver to see if he suddenly appeared from between the trees, and she put an extra effort into catching up with him.

'Nicky, stop at once!' Despite her attempt to sound authoritative her voice sounded flat and breathlessly cracked as she ran after him. 'Nicky!'

He gained the border of trees some yards ahead of her and she gave one last desperate shout, then closed her eyes in relief when the car stopped suddenly just short of him. In closing her eyes she momentarily lost her balance and missed her footing on the treacherous surface of wet grass, and before she had time to recover she tripped and fell to her knees.

She was not hurt, the ground was too soft to do any damage, but her tights were laddered and a great patch of wet mud adhered to each of her knees and to the palms of her hands when she put them down to save herself from sprawling full length. Her dignity was far more hurt than her body and she felt the colour flood hotly into her face when the car door opened and the driver stepped out to come hurrying towards her.

'Are you hurt?' Strong hands helped her to her feet and Rachel shook her head instinctively, startled to find that an arm was around her waist and a pair of anxious blue eyes were looking down at her.

'No, no, I'm all right, thank you.' She brushed ineffectually at the mud on her knees and hands and shook her head, looking across at Nicky, who now stood beside the newcomer with a broad smile of satisfaction on his face. 'Nicky——' she began.

'He ran to meet me,' the man told her hastily. 'I'm sorry, but he always comes looking for me when he knows I'm due to arrive.'

There was the faintest hint of an accent of some kind in the pleasantly light voice and Rachel looked at him curiously. There was a distinct likeness to Neil Brett too, although this man was better looking and his skin was fair and much more appropriate with that blond hair and blue eyes.

'You're——'

'Lars Bergen,' he said, and inclined his head briefly in a suggestion of a bow, a wide smile revealing excellent teeth. 'I don't think I've had the pleasure of seeing you before, have I?'

'Oh no, I'm new here!' Rachel responded to the smile automatically, but she was rapidly having to rethink yet again on the person of Lars Bergen. He was, after all, a grown man and not a little boy, and he was quite an attractive one too. She held out a hand which he took without hesitation and held for as long as she allowed it. 'My name's Rachel

Carson, Mr. Bergen, I'm Nicky's—I look after Nicky.'

'Ah!' The blue eyes appreciated her looks but with a less embarrassing frankness than Neil Brett had displayed, and he again inclined his head briefly in that almost bow. 'So Neil has at last found someone to care for Nicky—I am so glad!'

'Lars!'

Nicky tugged at the newcomer's sleeve, tired of being ignored, and Lars Bergen looked down at him for a moment before he bent and lifted the little boy into the air, swinging him round on to his shoulders with little regard for the effect of muddy shoes on a light grey suit.

'You should not run away from your pretty nurse, little one,' he told Nicky. 'Have you no more sense?'

Nicky giggled, looking down at Rachel with his blue eyes bright and glistening so that she had no heart to scold him for running off as he had. 'I was afraid you might not see him,' she explained. 'If he'd run out in front of you——'

Lars Bergen smiled, glancing up at the little boy on his shoulders. 'I'm used to him running to meet me,' he told her. 'He always does.' He looked at Rachel curiously for a moment. 'Did he not tell you he was coming to meet me?' he asked, and Rachel shook her head.

'No,' she admitted. 'Though he did say that Lars was coming, but of course it meant nothing to me at the time and I didn't know he meant now.'

Lars Bergen laughed. 'Children!' he declared

tolerantly, and started back towards the big silver grey car parked on the drive.

Rachel followed him because she felt there was little else she could do, but she felt horribly conspicuous with her mudstained knees and hands. It seemed she was likely to drive back to the house with them, but she would much rather have walked and crept in unseen until she was more presentable. Although her employer would no doubt expect her to stay with her charge no matter what the circumstances.

Lars Bergen opened the passenger seat door and dumped Nicky unceremoniously on the front side, but it left plenty of room for Rachel beside him, and the man stood by with the obvious intention of seeing her into the car too.

'Oh, I'd much better walk,' she objected hastily, and looked down at her muddy hands. 'I'm in such a mess!'

'It doesn't matter,' Lars Bergen assured her earnestly. 'Please come with us, Miss Carson, won't you?'

He was quite a bit shorter than Neil Brett, she discovered when she stood beside him, and much less disturbing at close quarters, but he was undeniably a very attractive man and quite disturbing enough in his own way. His blue eyes were steady and urged her to take the offer of a lift without further argument, and one hand was already under her elbow, persuasive in its own right as he stood waiting to help her into the car.

'Thank you!' She slid on to the seat beside

Nicky and he looked up at her and grinned in an oddly suggestive way that struck her as strange in a young child. Another smile from Lars Bergen brought a swift flush to her cheeks as he got into the car on the opposite side and slammed the door.

'Ready?' he asked, and Nicky nodded.

No one could have missed their arrival, for the long silver grey car announced its progress with an aggressive roar that Nicky found irresistible and copied as they drove towards the house. The distance was short, but it gave Rachel time to study the profile of the man who drove them, and she wondered if he really was Nicky's cousin or if he was more closely related to Neil Brett.

Nicky's mother, she remembered, had been Neil's sister, so it was possible that Lars Bergen was related to both of them through the distaff side of the family. As if he suspected her curiosity he turned his head as they approached the house and smiled.

'I should perhaps have explained,' he told her. 'I am Neil's cousin—our mothers were sisters, hence the likeness, yes?'

Rachel smiled. It was so easy to respond to Lars Bergen's open friendliness and she liked him instinctively, also she found him very attractive, though perhaps in a less blatant and earthy way than his cousin. 'You are alike,' she agreed. 'Though Nicky told me you were *his* cousin.'

For a moment he looked puzzled, then he laughed and nodded his head. 'Ah, you were expecting another little boy, hmm?' She nodded and he laughed again, his blue eyes gleaming warmly across at her above Nicky's head. 'I hope you are not disappointed, Miss Carson.'

'No, of course not,' she denied hastily, and he smiled.

'And since Nicky usually spends a good deal of time with me when I am here,' Lars Bergen told her, 'you will also, I presume, Miss Carson.'

The prospect was unexpected but far from unpleasant, and Rachel smiled. 'That might not be very easy,' she told him. 'Nicky said something about going riding together and——'

'Neil likes him to ride,' Lars Bergen explained as he stopped the car and came round to open her door. 'But he does not have much time to take him himself, so Nicky looks forward to my visits.' The blue eyes looked down at her, briefly speculative, and he raised a questioning brow. 'Do you ride, Miss Carson?'

Rachel shook her head. 'No, I'm afraid I don't.'

'A pity!' He led the way up the steps to the house and from the way he simply walked in it was evident that he was a frequent and welcome visitor. 'Ah, Mrs. Handley!' He greeted the housekeeper with a smile and indicated his parked car with one hand. 'Will you ask Handley to take up my luggage and put away the car for me, please?'

'Of course, sir.'

It was difficult to be sure, but Rachel had the feeling that for some reason Mrs Handley did not like Lars Bergen very much, and she could not help wondering why that was. She was not given long to speculate, however, for Lars Bergen went striding across the hall with Nicky clinging to his coat and Rachel saw little option at the moment but to follow them.

They walked into the sitting-room, Nicky clinging to Lars' coat and Rachel bringing up the rear, rather apprehensive when she realised that her employer was in occupation. So far, in the two weeks she had been there, he had been missing at lunchtime, and she and Nicky had eaten alone, a situation she found more to her liking, for sharing a meal with Neil Brett and having those icy blue eyes on her every move was disturbing, to say the least.

He got up and greeted Lars Bergen with a firm handshake, but even so there was a certain reserve in the welcome he extended his cousin, Rachel thought. As for her own appearance, he swept a swift and entirely disapproving glance over her mudstained hands and knees and raised one brow.

'Have you had an accident, Miss Carson?' he asked in a cool voice that suggested if she had it was most likely her own fault, and Rachel shook her head.

'Not exactly an accident, Mr. Brett,' she explained, and was conscious of Lars Bergen's eyes on her, curious and slightly narrowed. 'I fell in the mud,' she went on. 'I should have gone straight upstairs to change—I'm sorry.'

'Did you hurt yourself?' The question was so unexpected that Rachel stared at him for a moment and saw the hint of impatience in his eyes when she did not immediately answer.

'No,' she told him hastily. 'No, I'm not hurt, but I'm very dirty and I must go and clean up before lunch.' She half turned away, unable to face that steady scrutiny any longer. 'If you'll excuse me,' she said a little breathlessly.

'Take Nicky with you!'

She turned back swiftly, her eyes wide and, for the moment, uncomprehending. 'Take——'

'Take him with you,' Neil repeated the instruction with a certain slow precision, as if she was too stupid to understand his meaning, and she nodded, her face flushed with resentment at his tone.

'Yes, of course, Mr. Brett!'

Nicky, not unnaturally, was unwilling to leave his hero so soon and protested, clinging tightly to Lars' jacket. 'I want to stay,' he insisted loudly. 'I want to stay with Lars!'

'You'll go with Miss Carson now and come back when you have less mud on your shoes and your hair has been brushed,' Neil told him firmly. 'Now come along, Nicky, don't keep Miss Carson waiting!'

'Neil——'

'Do as you're told,' Neil insisted quietly but firmly, 'or you'll have your lunch in the nursery!' He looked at Rachel as if he expected her to support him, as of course she was bound to do. 'Miss Carson!'

She took Nicky's hand in hers, pulling him with her across the room, anxious not to have him make a scene. 'Come on, Nicky,' she urged softly. 'Let's go and clean up ready for lunch.' Nicky's bottom lip promised by its quiver to turn into a pout and his eyes had a bright and glistening look as if tears were not far off, but it took only a brief glance at his uncle to see that the order was unlikely to be repealed and Rachel's voice was gentle as she sought to console him. 'Come on, boy,' she urged quietly, 'come with me.'

She was far too occupied with getting Nicky out of the room with a minimum of fuss to notice the swift, sharp gleam that came into Neil Brett's eyes as he strode across the room after them and she looked up, startled, when he suddenly appeared beside her, his light blue eyes glittering down at her.

'Go on upstairs, Nicky,' he told the boy quietly, and Nicky, after a brief speculative glance at that set, stern face, went with only a minimum of complaint. When Rachel went to follow him, however, she was brought to a halt by a large firm hand curled about her arm tightly. 'Miss Carson,' he said in that cool, hard voice as Nicky went out of hearing, 'you will please not use that—that name for Nicky.'

Rachel, too stunned for the moment to follow his meaning, scarcely remembered just what she had called the little boy and she shook her head slowly as she stared at him. 'I—I don't understand,' she told him, and he frowned impatiently.

'You called him boy,' he reminded her shortly. 'I'd rather you didn't do so again!'

Rachel flushed, her eyes looking up at him

bright with indignation. To make such a fuss about a perfectly ordinary endearment seemed quite ridiculous in the circumstances and she was not going to sit down under such bigoted domination.

'That's quite unreasonable,' she objected in as steady a voice as she could manage. 'Surely a simple endearment used to a child——'

'It happened to be his mother's name for him,' Neil Brett interrupted harshly. 'You won't use it again, Miss Carson—do I make myself plain?'

Rachel was aware of Lars Bergen watching them from the other side of the room, although it was doubtful if he could hear much of the exchange, and she sought hastily for words to explain. Nicky himself had not been noticeably affected by her use of his mother's name for him, but apparently his uncle was, and once again she wondered what there was about his mother's death that made everyone so touchy about mentioning her or anything to do with her.

Rachel shook her head, seeking the right words, and briefly chanced an upward glance. 'I'm—I'm sorry,' she said, 'but I didn't know, of course, and——'

'You know now,' Neil interrupted shortly. 'I trust you won't forget again, Miss Carson!'

Rachel felt that the rebuke had been unfairly harsh considering she had done nothing so very terrible and Nicky had not been upset by it, and she challenged the instruction in this instance, whereas she would probably not have done in other circumstances.

'Nicky didn't seem very disturbed by my calling him boy,' she pointed out. 'Perhaps if——'

'Nicky isn't the only one concerned!' she was informed coldly, and there was a glitter of anger in the watching blue eyes. 'And I do not expect to have you debate whether or not my decisions suit you, Miss Carson—I expect you to do as you're told!'

'Like Nicky does?' she countered swiftly, and immediately realised how rash she had been.

Even through the thick sleeve of her jacket his fingers had a steely strength that made her wince and she fully expected to hear him say she could go and pack her things and leave immediately. Instead, after a second or two of shiveringly angry silence, he released her arm and waved a hand in dismissal. 'You'd better go and clean up for lunch,' he told her harshly, and turned swiftly to stride back across the room, leaving her standing there.

For a few seconds Rachel stared after him, unable to believe he had simply allowed the matter to drop, then, catching Lars Bergen's curious and rather anxious gaze on her, she turned and hurried across the hall and upstairs.

She must have been out of her mind to have challenged Neil Brett as she had, but somehow it had been irresistible, and the most astonishing part of the whole thing was that he had allowed her to get away with it.

Taking off her jacket in her room a few moments later, she curled her own fingers over the still aching muscle he had gripped so tightly, and shook her head. Neil Brett was just one more mystery in a curiously secretive household, and she had an almost irresistible urge to try and get close enough to understand him better.

CHAPTER THREE

NICKY was so anxious to reach the stable that he broke away from Rachel well before they got there and ran on ahead. He looked so tiny in a sweater and long trousers that were tucked into short riding boots that Rachel felt she would never have allowed him to ride if the decision had been left to her. The chances of falling seemed much too likely and as she was completely unfamiliar with horse-riding herself it had always struck her as rather a dangerous pastime.

A hard-topped hat eliminated some of the risk, of course, but even so it was quite a distance to the ground even from the back of a pony as small as Nicky's. The fact that Neil Brett was quite happy about letting him go, indeed he encouraged it, and that Lars would be in charge of him did little to make her change her opinion, although in the two days she had known Lars he had struck her as completely responsible.

The way down to the stable was a tree-lined bridle path from the back of the house. Bare-armed elms spread their huge gaunt skeletons against the cold winter sky and the narrow bridle path was wet and muddy after a night's rain, but the air smelled fresh and was tangily scented with loam from the shrubbery beside the path and the scent of wet leaves underfoot. The wind was a little less cutting this morning, but it still whipped a bright colour into Rachel's cheeks as she followed Nicky along the path and she was glad of a thick jacket over her woollen dress and the long boots that protected her slim legs.

There were three stalls in the stable, all of them occupied. A pair of handsome bay geldings were lodged in two of them and Nicky's sturdy little Welsh pony occupied the one nearest the door. Both Neil Brett and his cousin rode, though Neil's outings were restricted to the limited time he had free from running the estate and he had taken Nicky only once in the two weeks before Lars' arrival, but Rachel wondered if they ever rode together.

The tangy smell of the stable made her wrinkle her nose when she came to within a few feet of the yard and she could hear Nicky's excited voice chattering to Lars inside the building, anxious to be off. She had been down there only twice before, once when Neil took Nicky and yesterday when Lars had taken him, but she hesitated only briefly before going to the door.

Standing in the opening, she watched Nicky hovering anxiously round his cousin, chattering incessantly, and wondered at Lars' patience with him. Both men, in fact, were amazingly tolerant of his chattering and seldom lost patience with him, though the fact surprised her more in the case of Neil Brett than his cousin.

Lars looked up when she appeared and his blue

43

eyes warmed as he smiled at her, a smile that brought her sudden sense of well-being, as if the sun had suddenly come out. They had met briefly at breakfast, but there had been little time to do more than exchange good mornings because Nicky took all her time and attention at breakfast time.

'Hello again, Miss Carson,' Lars said. 'It's such a pity you can't come with us.'

He helped Nicky into the saddle, checking his hold on the reins and the length of his stirrups while Rachel watched a little anxiously as Nicky wriggled himself into a comfortable position. 'I don't really mind not coming,' she confessed, and instinctively called out a warning when Nicky dug his heels into the pony's plump sides and urged him through the doorway, making her step hastily out of the way.

'He's quite safe,' Lars told her with a smile that nevertheless acknowledged her cause for anxiety. 'He's very good for his age, Neil taught him well from the beginning.'

Rachel, who had imagined Lars as Nicky's instructor, looked at him with her surprise obvious on her face. 'Neil—his uncle taught him?' she asked, and Lars nodded.

'Yes—he would never have learned if he had to depend on my spasmodic visits.' He watched Nicky through the open door, much less anxious than she was about him, one arm resting along the top of the dividing panel between the stalls, good-looking, confident and completely at ease. 'Don't you really want to join us?' he asked, and smiled when she shook her head. 'But we'd—*I'd* love to have you along. I don't like leaving you behind.'

Rachel concentrated on the confident little figure of Nicky riding round the yard, content for the moment to go no further afield, and did not look at Lars Bergen who stood so disturbingly close. She knew well enough what he was trying to convey, not so much by the words he used as by the low, quiet tone of his voice.

'Nicky's quite safe with you, Mr. Bergen, I'm sure,' she told him. 'If Mr. Brett trusts you to take care of him then I see no reason why I shouldn't.'

He was close enough to reach out with one hand and touch her hair lightly with one finger, a gesture that sent a small shiver of anticipation through her and made her curl her fingers involuntarily into a ball. 'But I would much rather have your company,' he insisted, and lowered his voice still further, although there was little chance of Nicky overhearing him. 'And will you please call me Lars so that I may call you—Rachel, yes?'

Rachel nodded, her heart thudding hard at her ribs as she studiously avoided looking at him. He was a very attractive man and, although she had known him only two days, she already felt irresistibly drawn to him. Perhaps in part because he treated her with so much more gallantry than Neil Brett did.

What her employer would think about their rapidly developing relationship was another matter, however, and she was not prepared to risk Neil Brett's wrath if there was the slightest likelihood of his objecting. So instead of looking at him and giving Lars Bergen the encouragement he sought she kept her eyes fixed firmly on the little figure on the pony and tried to make her voice sound light and matter-of-fact.

'I've no objections at all, if you think Mr. Brett wouldn't mind,' she told him. 'In fact I'd like it, but if you think——'

'Neil?' She knew he was looking puzzled even without looking at him, and she saw from the corner of her eye the way his shoulders shrugged, as if he failed to follow her meaning. 'How can it concern Neil that I call you by your christian name?'

Rachel laughed a little uneasily. 'Well, for one thing, because I've only known you a couple of days,' she reminded him, 'and you *are* my employer's family. Mr. Brett might think that I——'

'Rachel!' He put a hand on her arm, not forcing her to turn, but persuading her with a light touch to look at him, and she saw that the blue eyes were warm and teasing, so that she wondered if he considered her slightly snobbish. 'What I do doesn't concern Neil,' he told her quietly. 'He leads his own life and I lead mine. Sometimes we do not see eye to eye, but mostly we get on well enough, and if I wish to be—friendly with a pretty girl then what right has he to object?'

'None, I suppose,' Rachel admitted, and smiled when she met his eyes. He had hesitated before describing his intentions towards her as friendly, but she accepted the fact that he had something rather more intimate in mind, and the idea was not at all distasteful to her.

The stroking finger on her hair touched her neck and she shivered involuntarily. 'There is no other reason for you being here than that of taking care of Nicky, is there, Rachel?' he asked, and Rachel looked up at him hastily, her face flushed warmly as she followed the implication all too easily, though for the moment it stunned her.

'No, of course there isn't!' she denied indignantly, and Lars smiled, shaking his head.

'Don't be angry,' he said soothingly. 'You do not surely imagine that my cousin is a monk, do you, Rachel?'

Quite inexplicably Rachel's heart was thudding anxiously at her ribs and she could think of little to say on the subject of Neil Brett's taste for women. 'I—I hadn't even thought about it,' she told him, 'and certainly not in connection with myself!'

'I'm sorry.' He was obviously anxious not to give offence and there was a hint of anxiety in his eyes as he looked at her. 'But you are a very lovely girl, Rachel, and you were troubled in case Neil should object to my—getting to know you better.' Again that delicate hesitation conveyed his meaning, and Rachel flushed as she shook her head.

'That was simply because I don't want to do anything to cause trouble,' she told him, 'in case Mr. Brett decides I'm not suitable to look after Nicky.' She glanced again at Nicky riding round the yard and rapidly growing impatient at the delay. 'I rather like it here.'

Lars put out his hand, just a thumb and forefinger holding her chin. 'But of course you like it here,' he agreed. 'And you'll go on being Nicky's nurse for a long time yet. Also,' he added in a low voice, 'you make this dull place so much more beautiful and interesting, lovely Rachel, be sure I shall do nothing to jeopardise that.'

Rachel's heart was beating rapidly and she trembled when his hand settled on her shoulder, the back of it strokingly gentle against her face. 'I think Seaways is lovely,' she told him in a light, almost breathless, voice. 'It isn't dull at all, certainly the interior isn't.'

'It isn't now you're here,' Lars agreed in the same quiet voice, and bent his head over her as if he meant to kiss her.

Rachel was not sure what she would have done if he had, but before he could accomplish anything a shadow fell across the stable doorway and the light was blocked by a tall, lean figure that stood for a moment, quite still, as if taking in the scene just inside the shadowy stable. Then Neil Brett brushed past them impatiently, a cold icy light in his blue eyes that sent a shiver running along Rachel's spine and made her catch her breath.

He did not look at them again, but lifted down a saddle from the wall and walked along to the end stall where the second gelding awaited a rider. Rachel watched him, her eyes anxious and almost unconscious of pushing aside Lars' hand from her chin.

'You'd better join Nicky,' she told Lars half under her breath. 'He's getting impatient.'

Nicky, in fact, was turning his pony to come back and see if his uncle was going to join the ride too, and he sat outside calling to him in his shrill small voice. For once his cries were ignored, however, and instead Neil turned swiftly and looked at Rachel, his eyes narrowed.

'It isn't necessary for you to whisper, Miss Carson,' he told her in a cool voice, and Rachel flushed.

'I—I didn't realise I was,' she said, inexplicably breathless. 'I was merely suggesting that Mr. Bergen joined Nicky before he grew too impatient.'

The blue gaze was immediately transferred to Lars, who hastily looked away while Rachel looked from one to the other uneasily. 'If you'd rather I took Nicky,' Neil said, 'I can, Lars. If you have something you'd rather be doing.'

The implication was too obvious to be ignored and Rachel noticed the bright flush on Lars' face as he glanced at her uneasily before answering. 'There's no need, I'll take him,' he said shortly. 'I was merely having a few words with Rachel before we left.'

As if to establish his right to do so he again put his arm along the top of the dividing panel behind her in a suggestively intimate posture. That and the use of her christian name sent one brow arching swiftly upwards to the sweep of blond hair across Neil's forehead, and he spared her a brief look before he again spoke to his cousin.

'I see,' he said quietly, and again Rachel detected far more meaning than the actual words conveyed.

49

It was evident that Lars too made a similar deduction, for his fair skin was still stained with that bright flush and there was a gleam in his eyes that resented it. 'I see no reason why I shouldn't talk to Rachel if I wish to,' he declared harshly, and Neil looked at him for a moment with raised brows before he answered.

'By all means speak to her,' he told him, 'but must you have your meetings in the stable, Lars—with Nicky looking on?'

Whatever was conveyed by the seemingly simple statement it was evident that it found a mark, for Lars' good-looking face betrayed not only anger but sudden realisation as well and his mouth was drawn tightly into a straight line. As if drawn by the tension between them Nicky rode his pony into the stable and sat for a moment looking from one to the other, then he looked at Rachel standing in the seemingly protective curve of Lars' right arm and blinked.

It was almost as if he had suddenly recognised a familiar scene and did not want to become involved in it, for he shook his head firmly as he turned the pony again and urged him back across the open yard, his voice shrill as he rode off, shouting out childish exhortations to the pony.

Lars' eyes followed him uneasily, a small upright figure confident but suddenly very vulnerable somehow, and he licked his lips anxiously. 'You surely don't think he remembers,' he suggested, and a short, harsh snort of derision cut him short.

'Yes, of course he remembers,' Neil told him.

'Didn't you *see* him remember?'

'But——' Lars shook his head, a whole gamut of expressions flitting across his good-looking features as he watched Nicky circle the yard again. Then he shrugged, a half defiant gesture that made Neil frown. 'I didn't think,' he said.

'Obviously,' Neil said quietly. 'But I'd rather you met Miss Carson elsewhere in the circumstances—at least when Nicky's around—I'm sure you see my reasons.'

For a moment Rachel thought Lars would simply agree and the matter would be closed, but his eyes had a bright defiant glitter and he glared at his cousin resentfully. 'You can't forget about Lynn, can you?' he asked in a harsh voice, and Neil looked at him steadily for a moment, his blue eyes narrowed.

'Can you?' he challenged.

For a moment Lars simply stood silent, staring at him, as if he knew for certain that every argument that came to mind was doomed to frustration. Then he shook his head as if to clear it, his mouth still tight and angry-looking, and without another word to Rachel he led the bay gelding he had saddled out into the yard and swung himself up into the saddle.

'Nicky!'

She heard him call to the little boy brusquely and impatiently, and a second later the two of them rode out of the yard, Nicky's voice coming back faintly on the cold autumn air, asking why his uncle was not coming too, and he turned as they went down the bridle path and waved. His uncle acknowledged the gesture casually before he returned to the task of saddling his own mount, taking no notice whatever of Rachel standing there.

It was not so much anger that gave the rugged features that cold, closed look, she thought as she looked at him through her lashes, but some other, much deeper emotion that she could not even guess at. The name Lynn had aroused such an intensity of feeling that it was clear she had made a very deep impression on both men, whoever she was, and Rachel's curiosity was aroused.

Lars had remarked that his cousin was not a monk, and one implication, as Rachel saw it, was that the mysterious Lynn had at some time been a bone of contention between the two men, although the thought of Neil Brett as a jealous lover was somehow oddly disturbing. It presented possibilities that had not, until now, seriously entered into the scheme of things and she eyed him again through the thickness of her lashes.

If Lars Bergen was good-looking and attractive in a more conventional way, then Neil Brett presented a much more serious challenge. His was a more mature and rugged sensuality that would be more difficult to cope with, should she ever allow herself to become involved, and she glanced at him briefly once more before deciding to leave him and walk back to the house. It was unlikely he would even notice her going, for he had completely ignored her once Lars and Nicky had departed.

Before she had taken more than a couple of steps

towards the door, however, he called out her name and she spun round swiftly, startled by the unexpectedness of it. Having called her back he said nothing for several seconds but simply stood and looked at her from the end of the stall, his gaze steady and unfathomable so that it was impossible for her to tell what was in his mind.

'You find Lars attractive?' he suggested suddenly, and Rachel flushed.

Her heart was hammering wildly at her ribs and she would have declared it no concern of his if she had followed her first instincts, but at the back of her mind she felt that he had some definite reason in mind for asking such a question, and instead she merely nodded and endeavoured to put her opinion into words that would not mislead.

'I—I think Mr. Bergen's very attractive and very charming,' she said slowly, and once again an expressive brow arched swiftly upwards.

He left the stall and came and stood in almost the same place that Lars had occupied a few minutes earlier, with his right arm along the dividing panel into the next stall. His light blue eyes were cool and steady as they looked down at her and he was much too close for Rachel's comfort, although she did her best to ignore the steady but violent beat of her heart that his proximity invoked.

'But you won't meet him again in the stable, as you did today,' he told her firmly, as if he had no thought of being contradicted, and Rachel blinked.

'I—I gather from your remarks to Mr. Bergen

that you—you have some special reason for asking that,' she said, and would have gone on, but he interrupted her, his blue eyes gleaming in the shadowy dimness of the stable.

'I'm *telling* you, Miss Carson,' he informed her, 'not asking you. You will not make your—assignations with my cousin here, and especially not when Nicky is with you, do I make myself plain?'

Mingled with the smells peculiar to a stable and horses was that tangy aura of maleness that seemed to envelop her, making her fingers curl tightly as she fought to still the emotional havoc he wrought. His blue shirt was open at the neck, despite the cold, and the strong brown length of his throat throbbed with life in a small pulse at its base.

'I—I was merely going to explain,' she said huskily, after a moment or two, 'that I was simply exchanging a few words with Mr. Bergen, as he told you. There was no arranged meeting and nor is there likely to be, especially as you seem to object so—so vehemently!' She looked at him briefly through her lashes, prompted by some sudden impulsive instinct she was unable to resist. 'I told Lars you would,' she added.

The blue eyes narrowed, looking at her steadily for a moment before he spoke, and she wondered if her defiance took him by surprise. 'You told Lars I'd object?' he asked quietly, and Rachel swallowed hard as she nodded.

'I—I told him you'd probably dislike the idea of my becoming too—too friendly with a member of your family,' she went on, and started visibly when

54

he removed his arm suddenly from the supporting panel and thrust the hand into a pocket.

He looked quite menacing, somehow, with his feet planted firmly apart on the straw scattered floor and that bright glitter in his blue eyes that she could not yet identify for sure as anger. 'So you think I'm a snob,' he said, and Rachel shook her head vaguely. Almost certainly if she annoyed him to the point of losing his temper, she would be out of a job, and she disliked the idea of that for several reasons.

'I—I didn't say you were a snob,' she denied hastily. 'I just mean that you—well, that you probably don't see things in quite the same light as Lars does.'

'That's quite possible!' To her sensitive ears his voice seemed to have a harsh timbre and she hesitated to meet the glittering blue gaze head on. 'Please don't misunderstand my interest,' he went on before she could say anything. 'I don't care how or when Lars conducts his affairs, just as long as he doesn't involve Nicky—that I will *not* allow!'

'There's no question of it being—of there being an affair,' Rachel denied in a small husky voice. 'And you have no right to imply otherwise!'

She felt appallingly close to tears and she could think of nothing more guaranteed to arouse Neil Brett's scorn than the weakness of tears. There was something unyielding about him that was new to her, and she found herself wanting to make him understand that there was nothing more than a mild flirtation between her and his cousin—at least so far.

'It doesn't concern me one way or the other,' he declared coolly. 'My only concern is for Nicky.'

'So is mine!'

Neil looked at her steadily for a moment, then he shook his head. 'I doubt it very much,' he argued confidently. 'No young girl as pretty as you can give her whole attention to a small boy when there's a man like Lars around to distract her.'

'That isn't true!' Rachel denied it breathlessly, but even to her own ears the denial sounded unconvincing. So far she had not allowed Lars Bergen to distract her at the expense of Nicky, but it was a possibility there was no denying, no matter how reluctant she was to admit it.

Neil swept a bold blue gaze over her slowly until her face burned with colour and it was plain he paid little heed to her denials. His wide straight mouth twitched for a moment in a hint of smile. 'Of course knowing that Lars would be coming here sooner or later,' he said, 'I should probably have taken a leaf out of your first interviewer's book and told you that you weren't suitable.'

Rachel's eyes glowed indignantly. Lars had said plainly that his cousin was no monk and here he was making remarks that implied her only distraction was likely to be Lars. It was too much to let it simply pass without comment and she allowed her need to hit back to override discretion as she curled her hands tightly and glared at him.

'Isn't that rather like the pot calling the kettle black?' she suggested rashly, and caught her breath when she saw the bright glitter in his eyes.

Her head swam with a chaos of speculation and her pulses were racing wildly as he stood and looked at her in a way that brought unfamiliar emotions into being. His tall, virile leanness was close enough to emanate a warmth that almost touched her own body and there seemed to be a curious hint of menace in the way he stood so that she shivered involuntarily.

'And what exactly does that imply?' he asked, and Rachel shook her head, unable and unwilling to say anything to make matters worse. The blue eyes quizzed her narrowly. 'Have you any complaints about the way I've behaved?' he asked, and once more Rachel shook her head.

'No,' she whispered. 'No, of course not!'

'Then I can only assume your remark was prompted by something that Lars had said,' he told her, and fixed her again with a steady gaze. 'Is that right?'

'No!' Rachel denied hastily, then bit her lip anxiously when he raised a doubting brow. 'He—Lars simply said that—that you weren't a monk,' she told him.

Neil half smiled. 'Did you think I was?' he asked, and Rachel realised suddenly that she was shaking her head.

'Good,' he said dryly, 'I'd hate to have you labour under a delusion!'

'Mr. Brett——'

'Do you want me to prove it?' he suggested, a bright glitter of challenge in his blue eyes, then he laughed shortly when the sudden shifting of his booted feet in the stable straw startled her into gasping aloud. 'You'd better go back to the house,' he said, shaking his head, and Rachel stared after him when he turned and walked back to the end stall, her eyes wide and slightly dazed.

His response to her jibe had been both unexpected and unnerving and she could feel herself trembling like a leaf, her legs almost too unsteady to do as he said and go back to the house. Instead she followed the broad back as he walked away from her and shook her head slowly.

'I'm—I'm sorry,' she ventured. 'I—I didn't mean to be—to be——'

'Provocative?' he suggested, turning to look at her over one shoulder, and Rachel shook her head hastily.

'I'm sorry.'

His face was shadowed in the dimly lit stall, his forehead half concealed by that swath of blond hair, and Rachel thought she had never seen anyone who looked more virile and masculine. Then he half smiled and it glittered and gleamed in his eyes as he looked at her.

'You might well be,' he said quietly, 'if you don't do as I say and go back to the house.'

He turned away again and once more Rachel looked at the broad, strong back presented to her. She looked at it for several seconds, half hoping he would look around again, then she turned without another word and went out of the stable, her heart still thudding heavily at her ribs as she went.

When she looked back, a few moments later he was riding out of the stable yard, following the same direction that Lars and Nicky had taken. A tall, lean, autocratic figure that stirred her pulses into response again so that she sighed resignedly as she made her way back to the house.

CHAPTER FOUR

LARS had taken Nicky riding with him and consequently Rachel found herself at rather a loose end. Several times during the past week, while Lars had been there, she had wished she could ride so that she could have gone with him too, but it was unlikely that Neil would look very kindly on any attempt of Lars' to teach her to ride when she was doing so in his time and on one of his horses.

More by instinct than deliberation Rachel had walked in the direction of the sea, something which she assumed was permissible when Nicky was not with her. Round by the road the distance was a little over two miles, but by walking over the fields as she had done it was rather less than a mile and Rachel felt a thrill of pleasure when she climbed over a wooden fence and found herself suddenly and almost unexpectedly on the top of some cliffs, bleak and cold at this time of year, but with a refreshing tang of salt in the air and the gulls screeching and swooping over the grey water its impact was exciting.

Being forbidden to bring Nicky anywhere near the sea she had so far not been herself, although there had been opportunities when she could have come, but the pleasure of it was all the more intense for having been delayed and she stood for a moment and enjoyed the sense of freedom it gave her.

There was a cold wind, but she was warmly clad and the brisk freshness of it whipped bright colour into her face and blew her dark hair back from her face where it was not confined to the red woollen hat she wore. Her thick woollen jacket had a high fur-fronted collar and she pulled it up around her ears as she started to walk.

The sea was rough too, churned into a white foam where it broke on the sandy beach, hissing and roaring noisily even at that distance, grey and menacing. But there was something irresistible about it too that never failed to stir her blood and seeing it in winter was a new experience for her. It looked grey and cold but much more exciting than the bright calm of summer, and she felt drawn to it as never before.

The cliffs were steep and chalky, topped by the short springy turf that characterises chalk downs, but further along she could see a place where the face of the cliff sloped sharply downwards, a break perhaps brought about by a past fall of chalk, and she considered the possibility of making use of it. She had plenty of time before she need get back and she knew from experience that Lars would have no objection to extending his baby-sitting duties even if she was a little later than expected.

After several hours of rain the day before the broken chalk on the downward climb was slippery where it had grown over with turf and Rachel had to pause several times to make certain of her next step before she went on. Perhaps she had been a little reckless to climb down to the beach when conditions were so far from perfect, but the sight and sound of the sea so close made the effort worthwhile and she went on. It seemed so long since she had visited the coast, and the certain knowledge that Nicky was in good hands gave her the freedom of mind to enjoy herself.

Once down on the beach she found there was less room for walking than she had anticipated, but a strip of several yards was enough to enjoy a brisk walk before climbing back to the top of the cliff again, and she thrust her gloved hands into her jacket pockets and went on happily. She would go only as far as the place where the cliffs curved outwards to form a natural bay, that would be well within her scope.

There was no sound but the roar of the wind-lashed water and the wind itself whistling across the narrow beach, and Rachel could imagine she was in another world. A world inhabited only by the screaming gulls and her own solitary figure walking along the strip of damp sand with the towering white chalk cliffs beside her, completely hiding any sign of civilisation and throwing back the sound of the sea like a defiant answer to its roar.

Only briefly did she remember that Nicky's mother had been drowned somewhere along this same rugged coastline, for she had no intention of putting herself into a position where the same thing could happen to her. Soon warm and glowing from her walk, she glanced suddenly at her watch, and realised it was time she started back. Nicky and Lars were probably already back from their ride and although she had no fears of Lars objecting, she preferred to be there to take charge of Nicky and get him ready for lunch in good time.

Turning back brought the wind slightly more in her favour and the return journey should be both quicker and less of a battle. She had gone several yards on her way back, watching the waves breaking on the shore only a few feet from where she was walking, when she noticed that the tide had turned.

In places her outward footprints which had been safely above the waterline were now being washed over by the incoming tide and erased, and it was only then, when she realised the significance of it, that she looked directly ahead at the way back to her point of access to the beach. With incredulous dismay she saw that her way was already blocked and only a few feet ahead of her the water was even now foaming right to the foot of the cliffs.

Not quite believing at first that it could actually have happened, she walked on, staring at the encroaching tide that every minute lapped more determinedly at the foot of the chalky cliffs. The beach was slightly wider in the spot she stood at the moment, but it lessened with every step she took and a hasty look back revealed no hope of access from it by any other means than the way she had come down.

Her situation, as far as she could see it, was not only hopeless but dangerous too, for being im-

mersed in the sea with the temperature at its
present level could guarantee severe exposure at
the least and probably worse if no one saw her
struggles. It was then that she once more remembered Nicky's mother and her blood ran cold when
she thought of herself suffering the same fate because she had been careless enough to take chances
with a strange environment.

Determinedly stifling a rising panic, she hurried
along the remaining stretch of sand left to her and
stopped only when she reached the swirling edge of
the water that cut off any further advance. So far
the tide only just covered the way through, but she
had no way of knowing how long it would be before it became deep enough to sweep her off her
feet, and she could not possibly attempt to swim
dressed in boots and a heavy wool jacket.

To dispense with them in the blustering east
wind would be just as rash and eventually she
decided to take what appeared to be the less un-
comfortable and dangerous course. It was only a
matter of about a hundred yards to where the
broken cliff gave access to safety and she felt she
had no option but to try and get there before the
water got any deeper.

Gritting her teeth, Rachel walked on into the
swirling tide, gasping anxiously when the receding
waves dragged at the sand under her feet and
almost made her fall. She used the cold slippery
surface of the soft chalk to help support her, but it
was of little use a moment later when the sea came
on again and this time threw a foam-edged wall of

water at her with such force that she staggered and fell, panting for breath.

The sheer icy coldness of it made recovery difficult and Rachel simply clung to the chalk as best she could while the receding water dragged at her, trying to break her hold and draw her under. 'Help!' She heard her own voice as if from a distance and knew she had almost no hope of being heard, but the need to cry out, however vainly, was undeniable. Added to the coldness of salt water that lashed into her face was the briefer warm saltiness of her own tears and she closed her eyes briefly in a silent prayer.

After what seemed like an eternity she opened her eyes again, blinking the clinging salt water from her lashes, and saw that a little way above her head was at least part of the answer to her prayer. The cliff face was not as completely smooth as it at first appeared, and about two feet or more above her a small, pitifully narrow ledge was cut into the white chalk.

Hardly daring to believe it at first, Rachel stared up at it, then pulling herself round to face the cliff she gazed up for several seconds while the sea again flung cold, angry waves at her to try and break her hold. She shook her head, her hands clinging determinedly, then with enormous effort reached up for the edge of the ledge.

Her gloved hands groped in vain the first time, but a second determined effort had her almost there until a huge wave flowed swiftly along from behind her and flung her off her feet, lifting her into the air and hurling her against the cliff.

Her scream of terror was drowned in the roar of the water, but when the terror subsided and she lay gasping for breath she realised that what she had believed to be the frustration of her efforts had in fact been her salvation. Her lack of inches had made it nearly impossible for her to reach the ledge with her hands, but being lifted into the air by that huge wave had given her the extra reach she needed and her hands had instinctively reached for the ledge.

She lay for a moment, too frightened to move, then gradually the truth dawned on her and she ventured to look down where she had stood only seconds before, shivering and hopeless in a danger of being swept away by the sea. Now she lay with her legs curled up under her on the cold but blessedly firm surface of the chalk ledge, and she closed her eyes, letting the warmth of tears run down her cheeks and turn chill in the blustering wind.

She dared not yet face the fact that she was very little better off than she had been before, but at least she was safe for the time being and she could only hope that the tide did not come up high enough to make even her present place of safety hazardous.

It was barely credible that her watch was still working, but a glance at it revealed that it was indeed still going and she realised for the first time that soon she would be missed. Someone, probably Lars, would realise that she would not have stayed out without saying so beforehand, and some effort would be made to find her. Whether or not they would think of looking for her on a small ledge above the sea remained to be seen, but the thought of someone missing her was comfort enough at the moment, and she sat back briefly and savoured her moment of relief.

The wind was bitter and Rachel shivered in her soaking wet clothes. An hour on the chalk ledge had seemed like twice as long and she had given up hope of anyone finding her. Instead she sat with her arms folded across her chest and her frozen hands tucked under her arms, shivering uncontrollably.

The wind whistled fiercely and the shrill cries of the gulls mocked her shattered nerves until she felt she hated them. She had cried for a while, but it had done nothing except briefly relieve her sense of hopelessness, and now she simply huddled against the wet chalk cliff and endured the shuddering cold and the relentless sound of the wind and the gulls while the hungry tide licked around her narrow refuge, spraying her with its chilling spindrift.

In a half stupor Rachel opened her eyes suddenly when she caught another sound above those she had endured for so long, a sound that made her heart jolt into violent activity as she strained her ears to listen. It was difficult to be sure, for even her own heartbeat contributed to the defeating jumble of sounds that deafened her to anything as faint as a human voice.

'Rachel!'

She stumbled clumsily to her feet, almost toppling over into the sea as she coped with a voice that souned pathetically inadequate against the wind and the sea. 'Here!' she called, her voice shaking. 'I'm down here!'

As yet she could not identify the owner of the voice, but it mattered little as long as she was found and she stood up, stretching as far as she was able with safety to call to whoever it was on the cliff top. It seemed incredible that anyone could have thought of looking for her in such a place, but that did not matter either, she simply wanted to be heard.

'Please, please don't go away!' she cried, her voice shrill with panic. 'I'm down here—on the cliff face!'

'Rachel?'

The hint of query made it obvious that she had been heard and she spared a second to close her eyes in relief before shouting again. 'Down here—on the cliff!'

The blond head could have belonged to either Lars or Neil, but those rugged brown features could belong only to Neil, and Rachel felt a warm and oddly elated sense of relief when she looked up at him. Obviously lying full length on the cliff top. he looked down at her for a second before he said anything, then his strong voice came down to her, surprisingly audible on the blustering wind.

'Sit back and wait,' he instructed with characteristic brevity. 'I'll be back for you!'

'Neil!'

Her cry echoed the panic she felt when his head vanished from her view and he immediately appeared again, his hands and shoulders visible this time too, bulky in a thick sheepskin jacket that looked blessedly warm.

'I'm going for a boat!' The words that reached her were distorted by the wind, almost snatched away before they were formed, but they were comforting in their certainty. 'Don't panic, just sit back and wait—I'll be back for you!'

Dumbly Rachel nodded, but her heart lurched alarmingly when he once again disappeared from view and she stared for a long time at the yawn of grey winter sky above the grass edge of the cliff where he had been. Then, shivering and soaked to the skin, she sat down on the ledge again, huddling against the wet chalk and wondering at the unexpected glow of warmth that ran over her chilled body suddenly.

Never in the month she had been at Seaways, no matter how often Lars used her christian name, had Neil Brett addressed her as anything less formal than Miss Carson, not even when it was not necessary to impress Nicky with a sense of propriety. It might almost be worthwhile being half-drowned and flung on to a cold wet ledge of rock to freeze if it achieved a less formal approach on the part of her employer, and unbelievably she found herself smiling.

More than half an hour—Rachel looked again at

her wristwatch in despair and hugged herself tightly to try and get more warmth into her chilled bones. She had never felt more wretched in her life and she had begun to doubt if Neil Brett meant to come back for her, although she knew at the back of her mind that the idea of his simply leaving her there was ridiculous.

The wind had already sapped what little bit of optimism the promised rescue had brought her and she was again steeped in self-pity when she caught the first sound of an outboard motor. It was coming from her left, at least she thought it was; with so many other sounds around her it was difficult to tell.

Then suddenly it came into view—a small motor launch, its outboard chugging healthily and a wave of white foam parting before it as it skimmed across the choppy grey water towards her. It took her only seconds to spot Neil's blond head in the cockpit beside a shorter, darker man and she once more felt the uncontrollable saltiness of tears rolling down her cheeks as she watched the approach with hazy eyes.

It was only now, as she watched the little boat coming rapidly nearer, that Rachel realised the possibility of Neil being angry about the trouble he had been put to. She had been rash, she was prepared to admit that much, but nothing more, and she wondered whether he would be willing to make allowances. Wondering about his reaction momentarily took some of the joy out of her rescue and she watched the approaching boat anxiously.

Neil looked a big and over-awing figure with the sheepskin jacket flying open over a thick sweater and he stood in the small boat in an attitude that somehow suggested aggressiveness. The other man was a stranger to her, presumably the owner of the boat, but she was glad of his presence as a deterrent to any outburst of anger on her employer's part, for even as much as she could see of him so far made her certain he was angry.

The boat, bobbing on the churning tide, looked in danger of being smashed against the chalky cliffs but skilful handling kept it at a safe distance and at the same time brought it close enough for Neil to reach up his hands for her.

'Jump!' he instructed, but Rachel, now that it came to the point, hesitated.

It looked a dismayingly long way down to the boat and the sea was rocking it so wildly that she had a sudden terror of being plunged again into that icy water. She shook her head, shrinking back against the cliff face, her eyes wide and frightened, too numb even to accept the assurance of those large and helpful hands outstretched to her.

'For God's sake, Rachel, jump!' Neil told her shortly. 'I can't climb up there for you, there isn't room, you'll have to jump!'

Rachel licked her lips nervously. 'I—I can't.'

'Yes, you can, now come on!' He reached up again and his hands slid beneath her arms as she bent towards him, a sudden blessed warmth flowing into her. She closed her eyes and tears trickled from between her long lashes as she jumped blindly, instinctively, not knowing if the rocking boat would receive her sudden unsteady weight or not.

The boat rocked wildly, spray hurling in over the side while the boatman did his best to steady it, and Neil's hands still held her firmly, safely, as she fought to keep her balance. 'O.K., miss?' The strange voice made her turn swiftly and she looked at the short dark figure of the boatman blankly for a moment, then nodded, still not daring to speak. 'Good!' the man said cheerfully. 'We'll soon have you back home now!'

Rachel simply nodded again. Her brain, like her body, was too numbed with cold and the stark reaction of fear to respond more fully and she simply stood there in the cockpit of the little boat like a small, bedraggled urchin. Then suddenly, without realising she was doing it, she swayed against the solid warmth of Neil, her hands clutching him tightly.

His arms took her hesitantly at first, then after a few seconds he suddenly hugged her close and Rachel felt herself trembling, shivering with a reaction that was both relief and response to the firm masculine body that seemed to envelop her completely as she pressed her face to the softness of his sweater. The open front of his jacket enfolded her like warm wings and she closed her eyes in the exquisite pleasure of emotional satisfaction.

He said nothing, but a few seconds later he gently put her away from him and she noticed a little dazedly that he did not look at her directly but rather concentrated on the task of removing his thick jacket. 'Take off that wet coat and put this on,' he instructed quietly, but Rachel instinctively shook her head.

'Oh no, I can't—what about——'

'Will you just for once do as I say without arguing?' he asked impatiently, and Rachel was aware of the dark man looking at her with a curiously speculative glint in his eyes as he guided the speeding boat back along the coast.

She caught her breath a moment later when Neil began to unbutton her wet jacket, stripping it from her without a word, then pushing her arms into the deliciously warm sheepskin, his mouth set tightly in determination. The boatman, Rachel noticed uneasily from the corner of her eye, was smiling, and as she hunched her shoulders gratefully into the thick, snug depth of the sheepskin, she wondered what he was thinking.

Glancing up at the tanned and rugged face of her employer, she blinked the last of the tears from her eyes, feeling suddenly and strangely elated despite the aching coldness of her body. 'Thank you,' she said huskily.

Neil said nothing, but she thought she caught a hint of a smile in the light blue eyes before he looked away again, and Rachel wondered if he had ever been as angry as she had supposed. He was watching the approaching shoreline and there was a curious air of satisfaction about him that puzzled her for the moment.

His car was parked on the quay not far from

where the boat landed them and he spared only a few seconds thanking the boatman, then hurried across the cobbled surface of the quay towards the car, but Rachel's legs felt too unsteady and weak to match his step and she hung back against the hand under her arm.

Frowning, he looked down at her and she felt ashamed of the weakness of tears, but there was nothing she could do about them and they coursed down her cold cheeks unchecked. 'I—I can't walk so fast,' she said in a small apologetic voice. 'My legs feel—feel wobbly and I——'

'Of course, I should have thought of that,' he interrupted hastily. 'It's reaction, naturally!' He did not hesitate a second longer, but lifted her up into his arms with an ease that startled her so that she instinctively put an arm round his neck and hung on tightly while he strode across the quay to the car.

Rachel was too stunned to say anything and he deposited her on the front seat as easily as Lars had done with Nicky, closing the door quickly and striding round to his own seat. There were so many things she wanted to ask about—like how on earth he had found her, but when he slid into the seat beside her and the warmth of his thigh pressed against her she could only stare ahead at the road and try to do something about the rapid and disturbing beat of her heart and the sensations he aroused in her.

She had no idea where they were, but it was obvious that he must have driven to somewhere along the coast where he knew he could borrow a boat and she realised just how much trouble she had put him to. So far she had not even thanked him for coming to find her, but at the moment she felt oddly shy and she simply sat there beside him with her hands drawn back into the warmth of his jacket sleeves, saying nothing as he drove out of the town and sped along a country road that she could only assume led them back to Seaways.

He looked warm enough in a thick blue sweater and even his hands, gloveless and strong on the steering wheel, looked capable of warming her own chilled ones and for a while the notion occupied her mind to the exclusion of all else. Realising how she was daydreaming suddenly, she shook herself back to reality and looked at him through the thickness of her lashes.

They were already turning into the drive at Seaways and she had still not expressed her thanks for rescuing her. 'I—I haven't thanked you for finding me,' she ventured in a voice that betrayed her uncertainty, and Neil turned his head briefly and looked at her.

There could have been a hint of smile on his wide, straight mouth, but she was not sure, and he turned away again before she could confirm it. 'I was the one who found you,' he told her in a quiet voice, 'because no one else considered you crazy enough to have gone near the sea in this weather.'

Unsure just how to take the bluntness of his confession, Rachel blinked for a moment before answering. 'I see,' she said, and to her surprise he smiled.

'I'm sure you do,' he said calmly.

'You haven't a very high opinion of my intelligence, have you, Mr. Brett?' She asked the question in a small unsteady voice that somehow sounded more hurt than she had intended it to, and he turned his head again briefly and looked over his shoulder at her.

'Your intelligence isn't in question,' he told her. 'But I happen to see you as impulsive and—rash, if you like; walking along the beach in the middle of winter would appeal to you, but it wouldn't even occur to you to check things like high water marks. I know you like the sea because you implied as much by wanting to take Nicky there, and when you were missing for so long it stood to reason that something had happened to you. Lars searched inland, I chose to look along the cliffs first—as it happened I was right.'

Rachel shivered, chilled again suddenly by the memory of her near disaster. If he had not thought her rash and impulsive enough to walk along the cliffs she might well have suffered the same fate as his sister had, and for the first time it occurred to her how much it must have meant to him to rescue her from that particular situation.

She looked at him through her lashes for a second, struggling to find the right words to tell him how sorry she was. 'I—I know how you must have felt,' she ventured. 'I mean, about having to rescue me from the—from where I was.' She was making a sorry mess of explaining, she realised, when she saw how set and withdrawn his expression was. 'What I mean is,' she went on hurriedly, 'I know that your sister was——' She swallowed hard, her hands shaking as she held them tightly together on her lap. 'I'm sorry you had to be reminded,' she finished huskily.

Neil braked the big car gently to a halt in front of the steps, then turned slightly in his seat to face her. There was a cool distant look in his blue eyes that made her shiver and Rachel curled her fingers anxiously as she hastily avoided his gaze. 'There was nothing I or anyone else could do about that,' he told her in a flat voice, 'and you have no need to feel guilty about anything—if that's what you're trying to say.'

'But I wouldn't have—I mean, I hate reminding you of something that must be—painful,' Rachel explained a little breathlessly, not sure that she was doing anything to help matters by trying to explain.

'I don't imagine you deliberately got yourself half drowned,' Neil told her in a cool voice, 'So you have no need to explain either. What you *do* need to do is to get into a hot bath and then into bed. Mrs. Handley will make you a hot drink and then we'll see if Doctor Corder need be called.'

He strode round the car and opened her door and Rachel let out a cry of surprise when he bent and lifted her into his arms. 'I can walk!' she told him, despite the fact that her arm was already encircling his neck, and he looked down at her with one brow raised. 'I can, honestly,' she insisted. 'And I don't need a doctor.'

Neil said nothing for the moment, but instead of standing her down he took the stone steps up to the front door with very little effort, putting her down on her feet only when they stood in the hall. Rachel slid her arm from his neck, reluctant to lose the warm, strong contact of his body, and for a second he stood looking down at her with a deep, unfathomable look in his eyes.

'After you've bathed and Mrs. Handley's put you to bed with something to warm you,' he told her quietly, 'then I'll decide whether or not you need a doctor.'

'But, Mr. Brett——'

He practically dragged her to the bottom of the stairs, then once more stood looking at her with that challenging gleam in his blue eyes, his hands turned backwards on his hips. 'If you feel you can't manage the stairs,' he told her, 'I can carry you.'

'Oh no, no!' Rachel urged her trembling legs forward and took the first step. 'I can manage easily, thank you!'

Neil nodded as if he was satisfied she was telling the truth, but he still stood watching her. 'Then I'll send Mrs. Handley up to you, and try and find Lars to tell him you're safe and sound,' he told her, and Rachel nodded resignedly as she started upstairs again. 'Oh, and Rachel!'

She turned, looking at him warily, finding his use of her Christian name strangely affecting in more familiar surroundings. 'Yes, Mr. Brett?'

'I'd like to be afforded the same privileges as my cousin,' he said in a quiet voice, 'so try and find Neil as palatable as Lars, will you?'

Rachel looked at him for a moment blankly, until she remembered her plaintive cry to him when she had seen him disappear from the top of the cliff. She nodded, her unsteady legs shaking with weakness but wary of being carried again because she did not know just how far she could trust her own reactions to him in the present situation.

'I'll try,' she whispered, and caught a glimpse of his smile as she turned away.

CHAPTER FIVE

ONE day's complete rest was long enough to effect a recovery and although the housekeeper expressed some doubt about her fitness Rachel insisted on getting up and returning to her normal routine. She had had nearly thirty-six hours of lying in bed and being waited on by a willing Mrs. Handley and she was tired of the inactivity, apart from feeling something of a fraud because she felt better after even a few hours and would have got up sooner if Neil had not issued instructions that she was not to be allowed to.

Nicky, she understood, had been told only that she was suffering from a slight cold, and Rachel could see the reason in that, for telling Nicky that she had been close to drowning would probably have had a much more dramatic effect on him that it had on Rachel herself. She was far too emotionally stable for there to have been any lasting effect on her nerves.

She went in to Nicky the following morning as usual and he showed a touching concern for her when she went in. His solemn blue eyes looked at her with an almost adult concern and he asked how she was without any prompting from the attendant Mrs. Handley, who had insisted on helping.

'I'm fine now, Nicky, thank you,' Rachel told

him, and gave him a close hug for his concern, realising for the first time just how fond she had grown of her small charge in the weeks she had been there. He was a fairly self-possessed child, but that curiously adult manner was somehow oddly endearing in so young a child.

'You got lost,' Nicky said, as if he knew all about it and, after a hasty glance at Mrs. Handley who nodded reassuringly, Rachel smiled agreement.

'Yes, I got lost,' she said, 'but fortunately Neil— your uncle guessed where I'd be and found me.'

'Neil said you was mad,' Nicky added with stunning frankness, and despite her effort to do something about it, Rachel felt her cheeks flush warmly with colour.

'Did he say that?' she asked casually, as if her heart was not racing so fast it made her breathless. 'Then I expect he's right, don't you?' she added, well able to believe Neil had expressed just those sentiments.

'He always is,' Nicky remarked matter-of-factly, and Rachel thought there was simply no answer to that.

When she came down to breakfast with Nicky, Lars expressed his concern more anxiously, although he was careful to omit any mention of the circumstances of the incident. His good-looking features were drawn into an anxious frown as he looked across the breakfast table at her, and he shook his head over her pallor.

'You don't look very well at all,' he told her. 'Are you sure you're all right, Rachel?'

Suspecting that Neil was more interested in her answer than he appeared to be Rachel nodded. 'Yes, of course, Lars, I'm fine.'

His eyes were a darker blue than Neil's and much less capable of concealing his feelings and he looked at her anxiously. 'You look so pale,' he insisted. 'Perhaps you should rest for another day or two, or at least take things easy.' He glanced at Neil. 'I'm sure Neil wouldn't mind in the circumstances.'

Neil looked up from his breakfast and Rachel hastily avoided his eyes, her heart beating rapidly at her ribs. 'The decision was Rachel's own,' he said quietly, 'not mine.'

'But you see how pale she is,' Lars urged, and Neil's blue eyes studied her for a moment, noting the pale softness of her skin and the darkness around her grey eyes.

'What about it, Rachel?' he asked. 'Do you feel you need more time to recover?'

His use of her christian name surprised Lars, and it did not please him either, if his slight frown was any indication, so that once again Rachel was driven to speculate. No matter what veneer of tolerance and politeness they put on their general behaviour, she thought, there was always that current of emotion between them, only barely concealed; passions she could only guess at and wonder what caused them. Almost certainly the mysterious Lynn whom Lars had referred to had something to do with it, and once again Rachel speculated on what kind of a woman could affect two such strong-minded men so dramatically.

Rachel blinked herself hastily back to reality when she realised that Neil was still watching her with a faintly curious glint in his blue eyes as he waited for an answer. 'Oh, I'm fine—really,' she assured him hurriedly. 'I don't need any more rest, I've already spent far too much time in bed as it is!'

After a brief, narrow-eyed scrutiny Neil nodded, apparently satisfied, but Lars was less easily convinced and was obviously bent on stressing her need for longer recovery. He reached over and took her hand, his fingers gently caressing, arousing her tingling senses to a response that startled her.

'But why not let me drive you into Mergeton, just for the ride?' he urged persuasively, and from the pitch of his voice it was safe to assume that he hoped to be inaudible to Nicky. 'It would be good for you to have a complete change of scene, Rachel,' he insisted, 'and I'd love to take you.'

It was obvious that Lars saw the opportunity as too good to overlook and meant to persuade her into going with him whether or not she was fit enough to resume her care of Nicky, and Rachel wondered whether Neil Brett saw through the plan as easily as she had herself—almost certainly he would. Whether Lars meant to include Nicky in the invitation she was not at all sure, but she doubted it in the circumstances. Before she had the opportunity to ask him, however, Nicky himself raised the question.

'Me too, Lars?' he asked. 'Me too, eh?'

From his initial frown it was obvious that Lars had not intended to include him, but he did his best to smooth over the fact by smiling at Nicky and winking one eye. 'You wish to play gooseberry, little one?' he asked, and Nicky laughed uncertainly, glancing from Lars to his uncle and back as he tried to puzzle the meaning of the question.

Neil said nothing, but he looked up and caught Rachel's gaze, holding it steadily as he looked at her over the rim of his coffee cup. It was a challenge, Rachel realised that, and one she could scarcely fail to recognise. Almost certainly he would not object to her going with Lars, but he was waiting to see if she took advantage of the opportunity to be alone with Lars or if she would stand by her declaration that she was quite fit enough to care for Nicky again.

'Lars is only teasing you, Nicky,' she told the boy quietly. 'We'll both drive into Mergeton with him.' She looked across at Neil, her chin unconsciously angled in a gesture that was as much defensive as defiant. 'Unless your uncle objects to us going, of course,' she added.

'Not at all.' The expression in his eyes was unfathomable, but it disturbed her vaguely and she hastily avoided it, giving her attention to Nicky while he disposed of the last of his breakfast.

'You run along and start getting ready, Nicky,' she told the boy a few seconds later. 'I'll be up to help you in a few minutes, as soon as I've finished my coffee.'

Only too anxious to be away, Nicky got down

from the table and hurried out of the room, banging the door behind him, a gesture that made his uncle frown. When Rachel turned back to the table Neil's eyes were on her again, their expression still cool and unfathomable, although a faint hint of smile touched his wide mouth.

'You need not take Nicky if you prefer to go with Lars alone,' he told her, and for some inexplicable reason Rachel felt her face flush warmly as she put down her empty cup.

It was as if he still challenged her willingness to take the boy and she resented it. Privately she was prepared to acknowledge the fact that she would have enjoyed a morning in Lars' company without the encumbrance of her young charge, but she had said she was ready to take Nicky and Neil had no cause to question her sincerity.

'Of course I'll take him,' she said. 'It's my job to look after Nicky, and I've said I'm perfectly fit again, Mr. Brett.'

'Mmm?'

'If you'll excuse me, I have to go and help Nicky!' She sounded a little breathless, she knew, but a raised brow had reminded her of her promise to be less formal and something in the depth of those blue eyes questioned her reasons for changing her mind.

'Rachel!' He offered no reason for calling her back as she got to the door, and she knew that Lars was watching, puzzled by something he could not understand.

She shook her head, instinct providing her with

an answer, her grey eyes holding his briefly while she stood in the open doorway, looking over her shoulder. 'I'm sorry, Neil,' she said huskily, and hurried out into the hall after Nicky.

She could hear his childish voice prattling to Mrs. Handley somewhere along the landing, so she had no fears that he would get into any immediate mischief and she took her time. That strange, indefinable air of unrest that characterised Seaways, she felt, was gradually involving her in its mystery and the thought of it was disturbing.

It was almost as if a restless spirit roamed the beautiful old house and the tension that existed between Lars and Neil served its unrest. Seaways must surely once have been a happy house, Rachel thought, it was inconceivable that it had not been at some time in its long history, perhaps even as recently as when Nicky's mother was alive, before she died so tragically last year. It was curious, she reflected, that no one so far had made any mention of Nicky's father, unless perhaps the explanation was the obvious and all too common one.

What was so strange was that an air of weariness and mistrust still disturbed the tranquillity of the old house and she could think of no reason for it. Nicky was a delightful and endearing child and not so far given to showing symptoms of the nervous stress that his uncle had warned her about, so there should have been little to cause the atmosphere that she daily became more aware of. Shrugging uneasily, Rachel carried on towards the tireless sound of Nicky's voice, resigned to the inexplicable at the moment.

To reach her own room and Nicky's she had to pass Lars' room which was on the same side of the landing, and as she passed it she noticed that the door was open. Most likely Mrs. Handley had been along, changing bed linen or checking on the progress of the daily woman who came in from the village, and she had accidentally left it open.

The temptation to glance in was irresistible and she did so almost automatically. Only a wardrobe and an armchair were visible through the opening, and a small bedside table on which Lars' gold wristwatch had been left carelessly abandoned beside a large framed photograph of a young woman.

It was probably wrong of her, but Rachel came to a halt by the open door almost without conscious effort and stood looking across at the photograph, a sudden and quite inexplicable urgency in her heartbeat.

The photograph showed a girl of about twenty-two or three, pretty in a rather childish way, with light brown hair and huge eyes. Her mouth half smiled and it looked both sultry and faintly sulky, and there was a look about her that was in some curious way familiar.

Seeing the portrait so prominently displayed by Lars' bed, Rachel was unable to resist lingering long enough to read the message that was scrawled in thick black ink across the bottom of it. *'Lars— forever, my darling, Lynn.'*

The outing had for the most part been enjoyable,

although Rachel found herself unable to forget for very long the portrait she had seen beside Lars' bed, of the mysterious Lynn. She wanted so much to ask about her, to discover just who she was, and mostly, she admitted to herself, because the girl had obviously meant something at some time to Neil Brett.

The girl had without doubt figured quite largely in the lives of both Neil and Lars, but it was her connection with Neil that interested Rachel most. She could not bring herself to ask about her and yet in one way she felt she almost had the right to, for Neil had compared her own situation with that of Lynn, whoever she might be, when he had ordered Lars not to meet Rachel again in the stable while she was with Nicky. Where Nicky fitted into the situation she had no idea, but that was just one more puzzle she must one day solve.

At the moment Nicky was playing on the gravel paths that wound through Mergeton's public park, darting between the bordering shrubs and shouting with glee when he emerged at some point further along. As far as Nicky was concerned the day had been an unqualified success and he was enjoying himself enormously.

It was cold but quite fine and a watery sun shone occasionally from behind the thick grey winter cloud, so that even the weather appeared to be on their side. They had lunched at a very expensive restaurant but abandoned the idea of going for a drive in favour of a walk in the park, mostly to please Nicky who got restless when he was confined to the car for too long.

There was something pleasantly intimate about sitting beside Lars on the green park seat watching Nicky chasing the birds who came to feed, but complete pleasure in the situation was denied Rachel because she could not erase those sultry but curiously childish features from her mind.

She studied Lars' fair good looks while he was engrossed in Nicky's antics and she tried not to think of herself becoming too serious about him. Not that she had inclinations that way at the moment, but if the sexily attractive Lynn had declared her love to be for ever then there was the possibility that he was not as free as he appeared. It might well be why Neil had more or less issued a warning, and she blinked in the sudden realisation that she did not even know if Lars was married or not!

As if he sensed her sudden tension Lars turned and smiled enquiringly. 'You're not cold?' he asked, and Rachel shook her head. Lars studied her for a second, then turned and faced her, taking her hands and looking just a little anxious, Rachel thought. 'Then what's wrong, Rachel?' he asked. 'I know there's something, you've been so quiet all day, and it's not like you at all to be so—so solemn.'

'I'm all right, Lars, honestly.' She had to admit he had cause for comment, for she had been preoccupied and she supposed he was entitled to an explanation, but at the moment she found it hard to put her feelings into words.

'You don't still feel—unwell?'

Rachel shook her head. 'No, honestly, I'm fine!'

'Then smile, hmm?' He leaned towards her and it seemed almost inevitable that he was going to kiss her so that she instinctively drew back. Whether it was because Nicky was close enough at the moment to see what they were doing and she had Neil's warning still in mind, she was not sure, but her reaction brought a frown of dislike to Lars' good-looking face. 'You do not want me to kiss you?' he asked, and for only the second time since he arrived she noticed that he had an accent.

Her brain was spinning, confused by a chaos of emotions and doubts, and she shook her head without even realising she was doing it. 'Lars, who is Lynn?'

'Lynn?' She felt the strong hands that held hers unconsciously tighten their grip and Lars' blue eyes looked at her uncertainly for a moment before he answered. When he did she thought his accent was stronger than she had ever noticed it, as if he chose his words with infinite care. 'Why do you ask about Lynn now?' he asked, and Rachel shrugged uneasily.

'I—I remember you mentioned her when you and Neil were talking in the stable one day,' she reminded him, and thought for a moment that for some curious reason he seemed relieved by her answer, although she could not imagine why.

He bent his head and studied his own fingers for a moment, twining them into Rachel's hair where it curled on to her shoulders. 'Lynn is dead,' he stated suddenly and with painful frankness. 'She was Nicky's mother.'

Rachel stared at him and her heart was rapping anxiously at her ribs, bereft of words for the moment. Not for anything now could she let him know she had seen the portrait in his room, nor that dramatic declaration of undying love. There was something much more complicated about the household at Seaways even than she had imagined, and she shook her head, wondering if Lars could possibly be as unaffected by Lynn's death as he appeared to be. It seemed impossible that he was, and yet he had made the statement quite baldly and with no sign of emotion.

'She was your cousin,' Rachel said, but he did not reply.

It was not difficult to imagine the additional complications involved with Lars and Lynn being first cousins, nor to imagine Neil's disapproval of the affair, so that she wondered if Neil had broken up the romance or whether Lynn's premature death had brought it about.

It also raised the question of whether Lars had been responsible for a break between Nicky's parents, but if that was so then surely it would have been Lars who was never mentioned in conversation, not Nicky's father, and Lars was still a welcome visitor at Seaways, despite that air of reserve between him and his cousin.

She sighed inwardly at the many unanswered questions that seemed to grow more all the time, and still Lars did not look up. Looking at his bent head Rachel felt suddenly sorry for him. He was good-looking and charming and it was quite possible that he had genuinely loved his pretty cousin.

It was no more than a year since the tragedy of Lynn's death and probably neither he nor Neil had sufficiently recovered from the shock of her death to look at past indiscretions dispassionately. It would explain their edgy and brittle politeness towards one another too, with both men mourning her, but for different reasons.

Lars raised his head at last and looked at her for a moment before he spoke. 'Would you like to go back?' he asked, and glanced at the overcast sky. 'It's going to rain, I think, and you must be cold sitting on this bench for so long, Rachel.'

She smiled, although it was quite true that the sky looked very threatening and she had become rather cold despite her thick clothes. 'It is turning chilly,' she agreed. 'I suppose we'd better think about going back.'

Lars pulled a face, grimacing at the gathering clouds. 'I dare not let you run the risk of getting wet again and catching pneumonia,' he told her with a short laugh, 'or Neil would never forgive me!'

Without warning Rachel's cheeks flushed warmly and she shook her head to deny any likelihood of his being blamed for whatever happened to her. 'It's very unlikely that you'd get the blame if I do catch pneumonia,' she told him. 'It's far more likely that Neil would say it was all my own doing for being such a fool, like he did when he rescued me from my last drenching!'

'Neil,' Lars echoed softly. 'I noticed the new air of familiarity at breakfast this morning!' He glanced over his shoulder to make sure that Nicky was safely out of earshot, then turned to her again. 'What exactly happened during that dramatic rescue, Rachel, that put you and Neil on such—intimate terms so suddenly?'

Rachel did not immediately answer him, but she got to her feet and called Nicky to her, her cheeks still warm with colour, although she refused to become indignant about the implications he was making as he probably expected her to. 'Nothing at all happened except that Neil saved my life,' she told him quietly. 'And after all, Lars, I have in fact known Neil for a lot longer than I have you and I already call you by your christian name!'

Lars got lazily to his feet and stood facing her, one gloved hand under her chin. It was hard to make herself remember that it was only a year since Lynn Browlett had died and that everything pointed to Lars having been her lover. He was so close that his mouth almost brushed hers and his breath was warm on her lips when he spoke.

'But with me it's different, surely, isn't it, Rachel?' he said.

Her heart was hammering hard at her ribs and the cold wind might have been a warm summer breeze for the glow that she felt, but Rachel was aware suddenly that Nicky was tugging at her coat and she looked down at him.

She saw that same anxious, vaguely uneasy look

that he had worn when he had seen her with Lars in the stable that day, in a position that suggested intimacy. He must have witnessed his mother in the same situation with Lars more than once, if Neil's hint was to be believed, and the familiarity of it troubled him as Neil had said it would.

Rachel put a protective hand on Nicky's head and half smiled. Heaven knew what would happen if she should ever become more serious about Lars, but at the moment she was more concerned with not letting Nicky see her as a painful reminder of his mother.

'We'll go home now,' she said.

Rachel had spent a restless night, in part because Nicky had gone to bed much later than usual and the excitement of a day out had made him restless. She should, she knew, have tried to quieten him before she put him to bed, but she had been rather preoccupied and so gave him less attention than usual.

She smiled at him now as she brushed his thick mop of brown hair back from his forehead. He was a good-looking little boy and very much like his mother, which was why the portrait of Lynn had struck Rachel as familiar.

With her mind brought back involuntarily to Lynn, she sighed inwardly. If there was a restless spirit at Seaways there was little doubt that it was the uneasy memory of Lynn, and her love for her cousin must in some way contribute to it. There was no way of knowing what would have happened if she had lived, but Lars seemed already recovered sufficiently to see Rachel as her successor. If Lynn had loved him as deeply as that message on the photograph suggested, it was no wonder her memory hovered like an unhappy shade over the old house.

'Can I go and see Taffy?' Nicky's question brought Rachel hastily back to reality and she smiled instinctively.

Taffy was his little Welsh pony and he sometimes liked to go down and see him before he had his breakfast, although it was a practice that Neil frowned on. Rachel sighed and pulled a face at his reflection, shaking her head. 'You know your uncle doesn't like you visiting the stable before you've had breakfast,' she reminded him, but Nicky thrust out his lip in a way that again reminded Rachel of the portrait of his mother.

'I won't be long,' he promised. 'And Handley's there, he doesn't let me get dirty, Miss Carson.'

Her hesitation was only brief, then Rachel nodded, smiling resignedly as she gave a last brush to his smart grey trousers. 'Just see that you *don't* get dirty,' she warned him, 'or your uncle will be angry with me as well!'

Nicky was out of the bedroom door in a moment and she heard him scampering down the stairs, so quickly that she held her breath until he reached the bottom for fear he missed his footing. She would have to take Neil's initial disapproval on her own shoulders, but the prospect did not worry her unduly.

Rachel went downstairs only seconds behind Nicky and as she went towards the breakfast-room door she heard voices raised—men's voices, easily identifiable even at some distance. Whatever they were arguing about Lars at least was making little effort not to be overheard.

Rachel hesitated, anxiously uncertain whether to go in and pretend she had heard nothing or to go back to her room until such time as the quarrel had burned itself out. It was the first time she had known them to quarrel openly and it was Neil who gave her the first inkling of what it was all about, speaking in his cool, firm voice and only just audible to her.

'Just stop and think before you get Rachel involved,' he told Lars. 'She's the kind of girl who'll take you seriously and she's—vulnerable.'

'Oh, nonsense!'

Rachel, her face burning with embarrassment, could well imagine Neil's expression at being so abruptly ridiculed and she bit her lip anxiously as she hovered by the door, seeking enough courage to go in. 'I'm warning you, Lars.' Neil's voice reached her again, as quiet as ever but with an icy edge to it. 'If you——'

'For God's sake, she's not Lynn!' Lars interrupted harshly, and Neil's response was angry and violent.

No longer caring whether or not it was ethical to interrupt their quarrel, Rachel was anxious only to put an end to the exchange before it became physical as well as verbal, and she opened the door suddenly and walked in. A heavy silence fell on the little room when she appeared, but the atmosphere was so charged with violence that she shivered.

As she looked from one to the other her heart thudded anxiously and there was a bright, anxious gleam in her eyes as the tip of her tongue briefly relieved the dryness of her lips. 'Good morning!' she ventured, but her voice trembled so much that it was doubtful if Neil, from where he stood, even heard it, and neither of them answered.

Lars stood by the long sideboard, his fair good-looking face flushed and his eyes dark with resentment. A hint of sulkiness pursed his mouth in much the same way she had seen Nicky do on occasions when he was denied his own way. It stunned her for a moment to detect anything so distinctly childish in Lars, and she hardly believed it.

Neil stood over by the window with his back to the light so that his expression was less easily judged, his rugged, tanned face half in darkness. His blond head was outlined by the winter sunshine behind him and its posture suggested a savage arrogance that would yield to no one. There was nothing even remotely childish about Neil and Rachel felt an involuntary shiver when she looked at him, her limbs weak and trembling with anticipation.

It was Neil, of course, who recovered first and he came striding across the room suddenly with an icy glint in his eyes and his features set like golden granite above the high collar of a grey sweater. For a second he said nothing, but his eyes moved swiftly over her flushed face and his mouth had a tight, firm look that betrayed his anger.

'Rachel?'

He had no need to put into words the question that was plain enough in his eyes, and Rachel nodded her head in a kind of breathless acknowledgment. 'I—I couldn't help overhearing,' she told him, 'but I've only just this minute come downstairs, Neil.'

'Nicky?'

She shook her head. 'He's gone down to the stable to see Taffy. I know——'

He waved a hand to dismiss the unimportance of such minor disobedience. 'How much did you overhear?' he asked, and she glanced warily at Lars, seeing him as the less violent one, though scarcely more reassuring.

Such intense passion as charged the atmosphere of the little room was something new to her and it disturbed her strangely, though not in quite the way she expected. There was a certain excitement about the situation that set her pulses racing and stirred strange and unfamiliar sensations into being.

Lars met her gaze briefly, but his dark blue eyes were wary as well as angry and resentful and Rachel wondered what had been said to provoke the quarrel, whether the blame had been his or Neil's. Then she flicked an uneasy glance at Neil's shadowed face before hastily looking down at her hands as she replied.

'I—I heard you warn Lars,' she admitted. 'That's all.'

'That's all!'

'Well, I could scarcely help overhearing some of it!' Rachel objected. Her eyes were bright and shining, defiance as well as a heaven knew what other strange and disturbing emotions shone in their depths. He had, after all, been angry in her defence, if the brief exchange she had overheard was any guide, and that knowledge gave her an unfamiliar glow of awareness as she faced him.

'No doubt!' He sounded as cool and self-possessed as always, and already, she guessed, some of the tension was going from him. Then he shook his head, his eyes icy cool. 'You'd better forget you heard anything at all,' he advised quietly. 'You don't need to become involved in private quarrels, Rachel.'

'But I heard you mention my name,' Rachel told him, and sought to steady her voice when she looked at him. 'I think that involves me whether I want to be or not. You really don't have to concern yourself, Neil,' she went on hastily, before he could say anything. 'I'm quite capable of taking care of myself.'

Neil's light blue eyes held hers for a moment, then slowly moved over her flushed face, coming to rest on the tremulous softness of her mouth. 'Are you?' he asked. 'That remains to be seen, doesn't it?'

'I—I appreciate your concern for me,' she went on, wishing her voice did not sound quite so small and unsteady, 'but I do know what I'm doing and——'

'I hope to God you do!' Neil interrupted harshly, then turned abruptly and strode past her to the door.

A tall, lean and infinitely disturbing figure—Rachel watched him leave the room with her heart thudding hard in her breast. It was intriguing to speculate why Neil Brett should take sufficient interest in her affairs to issue what amounted to a warning to Lars—intriguing and quite inexplicably exciting too.

CHAPTER SIX

IT was a little over a week since Lars had returned home to Sweden, although it hardly seemed that long. The day after he had quarrelled with Neil he had announced that he thought it was time that he went home for a while, although according to Mrs. Handley he came and went quite frequently, so the quarrel could have been quite incidental.

Lars had promised Rachel before he left that he would be back before too long, and she had no reason to doubt it. It was a curious thing, but she was convinced that, despite their differences and the suggestion of tension between them on occasion, the two cousins were genuinely attached to one another.

Even the tragedy of Lynn's premature death was a common bond and Rachel had wondered more than once if it was the ever-present shade of Lynn that brought Lars back so often. He was very fond of Nicky, of course, and that could be his prime reason for returning so often, also he was a confessed Anglophile.

So far Rachel had learned nothing about Lars' affair with Lynn, and the matter still intrigued her, the more so because Lars and Neil seemed to compare her with Lynn, a sometimes discomfiting comparison.

It would be scarcely politic to ask Mrs. Handley about anything so personal to members of the family, although it was certain she knew, but she was very loyal and very attached to Nicky and her employer. Possibly less so to Lars, but even so she was unlikely to gossip about any of them, and Rachel was obliged to remain in ignorance with the pretty, petulant face of Lynn constantly recurring in her thoughts.

Nicky missed Lars, although he was content enough in his uncle's company and Rachel felt sure that his love for Neil was much more deep and enduring than the somewhat lighthearted affection he had for Lars. Lars amused him, made him laugh and was tolerant to the point of over-indulgence, but with Neil he would sit in the evening before he went to bed, reading a book or chattering about the things he had done during the day. Their closeness during these evening sessions sometimes gave Rachel a curiously protective feeling as she watched them, a feeling she could not quite explain.

Her own sensibility concerning her employer and his cousin were less easy to define. Lars was amusing and charming and he made her feel very young and lighthearted so that she missed his company if only for those reasons. Neil, on the other hand, affected her in quite a different way.

Whenever she was in the same room with him she was tinglingly aware of his presence, of that aura of earthly virile masculinity that was impossible to ignore, and sometimes her reaction to him startled her. Whether Neil would have noticed her absence was debatable, she thought, but she was quite certain that Seaways would have seemed much less attractive without him.

She hastily brought herself back to earth suddenly when she realised that Nicky was running across the grass towards her, his childish voice calling her name and his face anxiously uncertain as he spread his arms and encircled her legs, hugging close to her.

Seeking a cause for his sudden flight, Rachel looked beyond him to where the tall bare oak trees lined the winding driveway up to the house and at first saw nothing. A second later, however, a man emerged from their shelter and started across the grass towards them, and Rachel took Nicky's hand firmly in hers, watching the man curiously, a faint flutter of suspicion making her eye him narrowly.

He was probably only a passing motorist seeking direction, but she had for a second felt a distinct sensation of doubt and she could not understand why. When the man came closer she could see that he was quite good-looking, although not outstandingly so.

'I suppose I'm trespassing?' he said before Rachel could speak, and she felt herself relax slightly at the sound of his voice.

It was cultured and pleasantly deep and had only faint overtones of some north-country dialect; as if he had spent some time in the south and almost obliterated his original vernacular with its softer tones. Rachel nodded, half smiling as she held on to Nicky's hand, aware that the little boy was now peering at the stranger, made bolder by her presence.

'I'm afraid you're trespassing,' she said. 'Are you lost? Perhaps I can help you.'

'Oh no, I'm not lost, thanks!' The man smiled and shook his head, then he looked across to where the leafless trees and shrubs allowed a partial view of Seaways. 'I saw the name on the gates and caught a glimpse of the house from the road,' he explained. 'It's pretty old, isn't it?'

Rachel smiled understanding at last. 'I believe it's Victorian,' she told him. 'More than that I can't tell you, I'm afraid. Are you interested in old houses?'

'Some!' He had eyes whose actual colour eluded her, but they seemed to be somewhere between grey and blue and they narrowed slightly when he looked down at the house again. 'Do you own it?' he asked, and Rachel laughingly denied it.

'I wish I did!' she told him. 'But I only live and work here—looking after Nicky.'

She glanced down at Nicky still standing close beside her and for the first time the stranger appeared to notice the boy. 'Hello,' he said, bending slightly at the waist to speak to him. 'So you're Nicky, are you?' Nicky nodded agreement, though somewhat hesitantly, and his hand clung even more tightly to Rachel's. 'Cat got your tongue?' the man teased and Nicky looked up at her anxiously.

'He's just a little shy,' Rachel explained. 'We don't see many strangers here.'

'No, I suppose not.' The man was still looking at Nicky, a glistening curiosity in his eyes. 'Aren't you at school yet?' he asked him, and Nicky shook his head. It was Rachel who answered for him.

'He isn't quite old enough yet,' she said, anxious for there to be no doubt about Nicky's intelligence even if he was a little unresponsible. 'He's five next June, aren't you, Nicky?'

'June, eh?' For some reason the man seemed to find the information interesting, unless he was simply being politely curious. He squatted on his heels and looked at Nicky with a persuasive smile, shrugging goodnaturedly when Nicky avoided his hand. 'And your mamma has a nanny to look after you, hmm?'

It was a bombshell Rachel told herself she could not possibly have anticipated and she drew Nicky close to her, a protective hand about his head as she looked at the man, knowing she could not blame him, but unable to keep a hint of reproach out of her voice. 'Nicky—lost his mother last year,' she told him in a hushed voice. 'His uncle takes care of him.'

'I'm sorry!' He looked again at Nicky, but Rachel felt that there was as much speculation as pity in his expression and she was puzzled by it.

'Why don't you run around and play again, Nicky?' she suggested gently. 'But stay where I can see you, won't you, dear?'

After a brief hesitation Nicky nodded his head,

then he ran off quickly, almost as if he was anxious to escape, and only seconds later he was making those noisy imitation engine sounds that were his favourite form of play. The man watched him for a second, then pulled a face as he looked down at her.

'I'm afraid I said the wrong thing,' he said, but oddly enough did not sound as apologetic as he might have done so that once again Rachel was puzzled by his manner.

'You weren't to know,' she told him. 'But Nicky's very sensitive about it still.'

'Of course.' He looked across at the house again as if he had lost interest in the child. 'I'll bet there's plenty of room for kids to run around in a place like that,' he remarked.

'It's beautiful inside,' Rachel said without commenting on its size. 'The outside doesn't really do it justice.'

For a moment the man's eyes settled on her, curious and almost speculative. 'You sound as if you like it here,' he suggested, and Rachel nodded.

'I do,' she agreed. 'I love it here!'

Again his eyes looked at her narrowly, speculating on her reasons for being so enthusiastic. 'Good boss?' he enquired, and Rachel saw no reason to deny it.

'Yes,' she said without hesitation, 'he's very good.'

'And rich too, obviously,' the man guessed with a hint of malice in his voice. 'The nearest I ever get to a place like this is by paying fifty pence to look around it.'

'Oh, I'm afraid Seaways isn't open to the public,' Rachel put in hastily, and the man laughed shortly, a sound in startling contrast to his pleasant voice.

'No, I can't see Neil Brett opening up his house to sightseers!' he declared, and for a moment Rachel stared at him, for she was quite certain she had never yet mentioned Neil by name.

'Do—do you know Mr. Brett?' she asked, and once again the man laughed—that harsh, humourless sound that Rachel found oddly disturbing without quite knowing why.

'I suppose you could say I do—in a way,' he told her, and she frowned.

'I don't understand——' she began, then stopped when the man shook his head impatiently.

'I don't suppose you do,' he told her shortly, 'but it doesn't matter—forget it!'

'If you called to see——'

Again she was cut short by that harsh laughter and blinked uneasily. 'I haven't called to see anybody,' he told her. 'I—well, I suppose you could say I was just curious.'

'About Seaways?' Rachel found it hard to simply walk away and end this rather discomfiting conversation, and somehow the man intrigued her and she tried to imagine what had brought him to Seaways if he had not called to see Neil or one of the staff.

He looked down at her briefly, then smiled and shrugged. 'Curiosity's my failing, love,' he said, and laughed again for no apparent reason.

'If you——'

Conscious suddenly of a dramatic change in his manner, Rachel stopped short and turned her head curiously, following the direction of his gaze. Nicky still played alone just off to their left, but it was not Nicky who had his attention, for while she still puzzled over it Neil's blond head appeared suddenly, plainly visible above the dark-leafed rhododendrons.

The stranger said nothing, but he watched steadily while Neil made his way round to the corner of the house, and once again Rachel felt strangely uneasy. The man had denied any knowledge of him, but it was fairly certain that he at least guessed who Neil was, and she felt more convinced than ever that she had not mentioned his name.

Neil himself obviously had no inkling that he was under observation, for he did not even turn his head in their direction and after a few seconds the man beside her turned, a curiously glittering look about him. 'That's your boss?' he asked, and Rachel nodded, horribly uncertain about answering so many questions.

'Yes,' she said, 'that's Mr. Brett.'

'He's the one who's looking after the boy?'

Rachel's heart was pounding urgently and she looked at him for a moment warily. 'Did—did you wish to see Mr. Brett?' she asked, and from the man's expression it was plain that he recognised the fact that he was being politely but firmly snubbed.

She felt badly out of her depth, dealing with this

itinerant stranger, and she wished Neil would see them, for he was much more capable of dealing with him, whoever he might be. Having watched Neil out of sight the man turned again and looked at her. There was a hint of smile about his mouth, but it did not reach his eyes and she shivered involuntarily.

'No, thanks, love,' he said, 'I don't want to see him—it wouldn't serve any useful purpose at the moment.' He inclined his head briefly. 'Thanks for the chat—it's been nice meeting you!'

Too stunned to reply, Rachel merely nodded. Then the man was looking past her, narrow-eyed as he watched Nicky running around with his arms outstretched, dipping and weaving, his mouth puckered and emitting imaginary engine noises, oblivious of everything but his game. Shaking his head, the man shrugged and walked off, back towards the trees along the driveway. It was only seconds after he disappeared that Rachel heard a car engine start up and she stood for a moment staring at the ribbon of bare-armed oaks.

'Nicky!' Suddenly anxious, she called him to her and they made their way back to the house, but the face of the curious stranger still lingered uneasily in her mind.

It was Nicky who first mentioned the man at dinner that same evening, and Rachel wished she had spoken of it herself, for Neil eyed her suspiciously, almost as if he suspected she had deliberately kept the meeting quiet. Not that Nicky said very much, but the brief fact that Rachel had been talking to a strange man in the grounds was evidently enough to arouse Neil's interest and his blue eyes regarded her steadily.

'You met someone in the grounds?' he asked, and Rachel instinctively shook her head.

'Not by design, if that's what you mean,' she denied. 'He suddenly appeared from among the trees along the drive—presumably he had a car parked somewhere nearby, because I heard one start up just after he left.'

'You didn't know him?'

Rachel shook her head. She resented the suggestion of suspicion more than she cared to show at the moment. 'I thought at first he might be a motorist looking for directions,' she explained, and Neil looked at her, struck by her choice of words.

'It's unlikely,' he observed, 'we don't get many stray motorists out this way.'

Rachel was tempted to tell him that the man seemingly knew Neil's name without her mentioning it, but on second thoughts she wondered if it was a good idea. She knew little about his past life and the man could well be someone he would prefer not to meet again. The man's whole attitude and his mode of reference to Neil had hardly suggested an amicable relationship.

'Maybe he *was* simply lost and he didn't like to admit it,' she ventured, but Neil frowned as if nothing so simple satisfied him.

'You said you thought *at first* he might have been someone looking for directions,' he reminded her. 'What changed your mind, Rachel?'

It was difficult being as frank as she would like to have been in front of Nicky and she glanced at him before shaking her head at Neil. He said no more on the subject, but a brief glance at him was enough to realise that the matter was only temporarily suspended.

It was after she had put Nicky to bed and came downstairs again that Neil met her in the hall. 'I'd like you to join me,' he said without preliminary, and Rachel nodded, although with some misgiving, for heaven knew what he expected her to be able to tell him.

Usually in the evenings when Nicky was safely in bed she sat with Mr. and Mrs. Handley in their cosy little room, or else she used the smaller sitting-room at the back of the house and either read or caught up on her letter writing. Only very occasionally did she join Neil in the big sitting-room, for she found him disturbing company at any time and more especially so when there were only the two of them.

The wind outside swished the branches of a tree angrily against the window and sharp scatters of rain beat noisily on the panes, but inside the big room was warm and comfortable—a cosy, inviting scene with a fire in the hearth flickering brightly and big, round oak logs sputtering into showers of sparks.

The only illumination came from a couple of table lamps and they gave a soft subdued glow that concentrated light only into one small section of the big room. Neil saw her seated in one of the deceptively frail-looking armchairs the room was furnished with, then he seated himself opposite to her on the other side of the fireplace.

The soft light from one of the lamps cast dark shadows over his rugged features and gave him a curiously graven look, as if he had been hewn from bronze, an illusion that was fostered by the strong tanned hands and forearms emerging from the sleeves of a light blue sweater.

The whole setting was so warm and suggestive of intimacy and the man opposite her so affected her senses that Rachel felt her pulses responding to thoughts that came unbidden into her mind and stirred emotions in her that she barely recognised. There was something so utterly familiar about Neil Brett and yet he was still virtually a stranger to her, a stranger that her instincts clamoured to know better. To get closer to the man she suspected he could be behind that icy façade.

Even in the few seconds she had sat there by the fire she had become so immersed in her own thoughts that she started almost guiltily when he spoke. 'You know what I want to talk to you about?' he asked, and for a moment Rachel sought wildly for his meaning. The very existence of the man she had met in the grounds had been forgotten in her preoccupation with Neil.

Then she nodded, bringing herself hastily back to earth. 'I—I think so,' she said. 'It's about the man—the one I spoke to this morning.'

He nodded briefly. 'Was today the first time

you'd seen him?'

Rachel blinked. 'Oh yes, of course it was!' she said, but Neil looked at her narrowly.

'You're sure?'

Uncertain just what he was getting at, she frowned. 'Of course I'm sure, Neil,' she told him. 'If you think——'

'I don't know what to think,' Neil interrupted shortly. The blue eyes held hers for a moment and she thought there was anxiety as well as a hint of suspicion in them, a suspicion that brought as much hurt as resentment. 'I don't know you well enough, Rachel,' he went on after a second or two. 'I don't know whether it's possible that someone—a lover, perhaps, could have found where you are and followed you here.'

Rachel stared at him for a moment, her cheeks flushed and a bright, dark look in her eyes as she struggled to see his point of view. A lover, he had suggested, and she almost laughed when she recalled that Lars had once tentatively suggested Neil himself for that role.

'A lover?' she said huskily. 'Would you expect me to have a lover follow me down here?'

For a moment the light blue eyes swept over her face and figure, then he nodded, apparently quite serious about it. 'Yes,' he said softly, 'I would.'

Hastily Rachel looked away, her heart thudding wildly. 'I haven't a lover,' she told him in the same small husky voice. 'Nor is it anyone else to do with me, Neil.'

'Then who?'

He spoke softly, almost as if he spoke to himself, and Rachel shook her head slowly. It was obvious that now he had excluded anyone of her acquaintance he shared her own initial suspicion about the stranger, although heaven knew why. A passing motorist should surely not cause such a furore, but the man himself had aroused her suspicions and she in turn had communicated them to Neil.

'Neil.' She hesitated and he looked across at her, his blue eyes darkened by the firelight. 'I did wonder about him,' she explained rather vaguely, and Neil frowned.

'You wondered?' he echoed, and Rachel shrugged, warily confiding.

'I asked him if he wanted to see you,' she explained, 'but he—he said it would serve no useful purpose.'

Neil looked at her for a second or two, his eyes narrowed as if he was trying to follow her exact meaning. 'You asked him if he wanted to see me?' he said. 'Why?'

It was difficult to explain to him exactly how she had felt when the stranger had so glibly used his name and she shrugged uneasily under that discomfiting scrutiny. 'I don't really know,' she confessed, 'except that—oh, I don't know, there was just something about him! He spoke about the house and I thought at first that he was lost and he'd stopped to ask directions, but then he said he was interested in old houses.'

'And?' He sounded impatient and Rachel shook her head hastily.

'I told him that Seaways wasn't open to the public,' she explained, 'but he knew that already. Also——' She hesitated, but went on hastily when she saw Neil's impatient frown. 'He knew your name,' she said, and Neil's eyes narrowed sharply.

'You didn't tell me that at first,' he said shortly. 'Why not?'

Rachel shrugged. 'I—I don't know—it bothered me, but——'

'I think you'd better tell me all of it,' Neil interrupted harshly. 'Where exactly was he?'

'He came out of the trees alongside the drive,' she told him. 'Nicky came run——'

'Nicky?' He barked the name at her so sharply that Rachel blinked. 'He spoke to Nicky?'

'Well, yes,' she said. 'Nicky ran back when he saw him coming.'

There was a definite air of tension about him, a certainty that had only been hinted at before, and Rachel felt her heart thudding anxiously when she looked across at him. His big hands were clasped together as he leaned forward in his chair, his elbows resting on his knees, and there was a taut, dark look on his face that aroused uneasy responses in her.

'Neil,' she began, 'do you——'

'Describe him,' Neil told her shortly. 'What did he look like, Rachel?'

'He was good-looking.' She searched her mind for details of the man's appearance, wondering at his sense of urgency. 'Not as tall as you are, more Lars' height—brown hair, quite dark brown and——

I'm not sure about his eyes, they were either blue or grey.'

Neil sat with one hand running through the thick blond hair at the back of his head and there was a tight, drawn look about his mouth, a glitter in his eyes that sent a shiver down his spine like ice water. 'Browlett!' he said in a harsh whisper, and Rachel stared at him. 'Michael Browlett!'

Her heart was racing so hard she was quite breathless with it and she looked across at Neil's shadowed and unfathomable features in stunned disbelief. 'Browlett,' she echoed in a daze. 'That's——'

'Nicky's father!' Neil confirmed harshly, and Rachel still stared at him unbelievingly.

She took a moment to wonder why, with all the possibilities that had passed through her mind about why the strange man was there, it had never once occurred to her that he might be Nicky's father. Why Neil and not his father was Nicky's legal guardian had several possible explanations, but what puzzled her was why Neil was so disturbed at the idea of the man seeing his son.

'I—I had no idea,' Rachel said. 'If only he'd said who he was I'd have——'

'You did exactly right to come back to the house,' Neil told her shortly. 'I hope you'll have as much sense again if the situation arises.'

Rachel looked at him uneasily, not at all sure if she either followed his reasoning or approved of his apparent determination to forbid a further meeting. 'Is he likely to come back?' she asked, and Neil shrugged heavily.

'It's likely,' he said. 'Until I can make some en-
quiries, Rachel, I'd rather you kept Nicky close to
the house unless either Handley or myself is with
you, is that clear?'

'It's clear enough,' Rachel agreed, beginning to
see things in a slightly different light now that she
knew the man's identity. 'But surely if he *is* Nicky's
father——'

She stopped short when she caught the glittering
look in Neil's eyes. 'I suppose,' he said in a flat,
hard voice, 'it's too much to ask that you do as
you're told for once, without question?'

Rachel curled her hands tightly, not at all sure
that to deprive a man of the sight of his son was
ethical. 'You won't—you wouldn't let him see
Nicky?' she asked, and Neil frowned warningly.

'Rachel! Don't interfere in things that you know
nothing about!'

'But do you have the *right*?' Rachel insisted
earnestly. 'He's the boy's father, Neil, surely you
can't——'

Neil got to his feet in a sudden, swift movement
that made Rachel gasp. It seemed to her to con-
stitute a threat so that she got up herself and stood
facing him on the other side of the fireplace, a
small uneasy figure with bright anxious eyes that
watched him warily.

'You know nothing about the circumstances,' he
told her. His voice was hard and flat and in chilling
contrast to the anger that glittered in his eyes. 'Just
do as I say, Rachel, and don't try to change things

when you don't know what the results could be!'

'You're telling me I mustn't take Nicky out into the gardens again?' she ventured, and he shook his head impatiently.

'I'm telling you to stay near the house unless either Handley or myself is within call,' he said. 'He can play in the gardens, of course, just as long as someone is within call.'

'I see.' Rachel tried to sound matter-of-fact, but in the circumstances it was difficult. 'It isn't going to be easy trying to explain to him,' she said. 'What reason do I give him?'

Neil's mouth tightened, as if he suspected she was looking for arguments. 'You simply tell him that he mustn't go running off alone the way he does,' he told her. 'He's obedient enough to do as he's told, surely!'

'Yes, of course he is,' Rachel agreed, 'but——'

She drew in her breath sharply when a strong hand reached across and curled itself round her slim wrist, the fingers cruelly tight on her soft skin. Drawn nearer to him by the irresistible strength of his grip she stood in front of the bright fire, looking up at him with huge eyes made dark by the shadows that surrounded them.

'You have a choice, Rachel,' he told her very quietly and speaking slowly as if he chose his words with care. 'Either you do as I say and stay close to the house unless someone else is with you both, or you go—right now! The choice is yours and, much as I know Nicky would miss you, if you can't bring yourself to follow instructions then the solution is in your own hands!'

To Rachel the ultimatum came as a cold shock and she found it hard to put anything into words. She simply stared at her own captive wrist, her eyes suspiciously bright with threatened tears, for she knew he meant every word of it. He would see her go with no regrets at all and it was that realisation, perhaps more than any other, that stung most.

'Is that what you'd rather I did?' she asked in a small unsteady voice, and for a moment Neil said nothing.

Then he shook his head slowly and she realised that the anger in his eyes was already less evident. 'I think you know that's nonsense,' he said. 'You're very good with Nicky and he likes you. Also I hate having to get used to new staff.'

They were all very good reasons, Rachel recognised, but they were so severely practical that for a moment she felt the coldness of disappointment. If only he could have made his reasons more personal, more gentle. He looked so tall and almost frighteningly earthy standing there in the flickering firelight that she felt her heart pounding like a hammer at her ribs when she looked at him.

Lars, she reflected ruefully, would have expressed his reluctance to see her go in quite different terms, and almost as if he guessed what was in her mind, Neil shook his head suddenly, a hint of smile on his wide mouth. 'Also,' he added, 'I should have to face Lars when he comes back and I'd find it rather awkward if you weren't here.'

'Of course!'

Rachel felt her pulses flutter erratically when the ball of his thumb began to move slowly and gently on the soft skin of her inner arm. It was an incredibly sensual caress and she scarcely believed it could be Neil who held her like that, although Lars had once implied that there was more to his cousin than she had so far experienced.

'Of course!' he echoed softly.

Rachel coped with another flutter of uncertainty when he smiled and suddenly shook his head. Almost convinced that she was the cause of his amusement, she snatched her arm out of his grasp and looked up at him with bright, reproachful eyes. 'I have things to do,' she told him in a small, unsteady voice. 'If you'll excuse me.'

He said nothing until she opened the door into the hall, then he called her back, though she came only hesitantly, her eyes wary. 'You haven't told me,' he said, 'whether you're willing to stay and do as I say, or if you've decided to leave. Which is it to be, Rachel?'

Briefly Rachel met his eyes and the challenge in them was unmistakable so that she instinctively lifted her chin in defiance of it. 'I'll stay,' she said, 'for Nicky's sake!'

She gasped aloud when he bent his head suddenly and without warning brushed his firm mouth against her lips in a warm, gentle pressure that ran through her like fire. 'Good!' he said softly, and watched with glittering eyes as she hurried from the room.

CHAPTER SEVEN

'IF Mr. Brett thinks it's best, then most likely it is,' Mrs. Handley said in her quiet country voice, and Rachel sighed inwardly at the inevitability of it. Mrs. Handley's loyalty to her employer was firm and uncompromising and Rachel wondered if Neil realised what a gem she was.

Rachel had been complaining, with no real malice, about having to stay close to the house all the time. It irritated her at times to have her movements restricted, and Nicky did not understand it either, although he was easily enough mollified when his interest was taken with something else.

'I'll be glad when Nicky and I can go where we like again,' Rachel said, and Mrs. Handley nodded sympathetically.

'I expect so, my dear,' she said. 'Perhaps it won't be too long now.'

Nothing so far had been mentioned about Rachel's meeting with Michael Browlett, but she had little doubt that Mrs. Handley knew all about it. She and her husband had never done other than work at Seaways and there was little that was likely to remain unknown to them.

In the time Rachel had been there she had become quite friendly with the Handleys, but never so far had anything made them change their reticent manner where the family was concerned. Rachel sat now in their little sitting-room next to the kitchen, talking to Mrs. Handley while Handley worked in the kitchen garden and at the same time entertained Nicky.

Watching them from the window and listening to Nicky's chatter Rachel recalled again the features of Michael Browlett, and she had no doubt at all that Neil had been right in his identification of the man, for there was a similarity between him and Nicky that was unmistakable in hindsight. It seemed such a pity, she thought, that they could not meet, just once, and recognise one another.

Of course Mrs. Handley would know all about Michael Browlett too, although it was unlikely she would be any more forthcoming about him than about anything else concerning the family. If she mentioned anything, however harmless it appeared, the housekeeper would revert to those monosyllabic answers she always did.

Unable to resist passing comment, for all it was useless, Rachel looked at Nicky and smiled. 'Nicky's like his father,' she ventured, but once again, as she expected, that invisible barrier was raised.

'Handsome little boy,' Mrs. Handley agreed, and Rachel almost laughed at such determined evasion.

With having her personal freedom restricted to some extent because of her meeting with Michael Browlett, however, Rachel felt she was now more closely involved and that she had a right to some answers at least, so she pressed on where at one time she would have fallen silent. 'I don't quite see why Neil—Mr. Brett objects so strongly to his father seeing him,' she observed, but realised her mistake immediately when Mrs. Handley took up arms in her employer's defence.

'Mr. Brett does his very best for the boy,' she declared sternly. 'It's not every unmarried gentleman would take on the upbringing of a little boy the way Mr. Brett has!'

'Oh, I agree,' Rachel agreed hastily. 'I think he's wonderful with Nicky, but—I don't know, it doesn't seem right not to let his natural father see him sometimes.'

Mrs. Handley's round homely face was flushed and her eyes showed an unmistakable glint of anger as she pulled back her thin shoulders and bridled indignantly. 'No natural father would 'ave gone off the way he did!' she declared firmly. 'That mite wouldn't have had no father at all if it hadn't been for Mr. Brett! Better than that feckless creature who was responsible for his being born, and who's to say he hasn't got the right to keep the other one away after all this time?'

Rachel was stunned momentarily by the fierceness of the tirade and she blinked at Mrs. Handley a little uncertainly. 'But even so,' she said, 'isn't Mr. Browlett allowed access to his son?'

'Why should he have?' Mrs. Handley demanded with a disparaging sniff. 'Nobody even knew if he was alive or dead until now, since he careered off before the mite was born and no one's heard of him since—it's not likely he cares much for him anyway.'

Rachel shook her head, stunned by yet another revelation about Nicky's background and wondering how much more there was still hidden. 'Do you mean he'd—he'd never seen his father before the other day?' she asked, and Mrs. Handley shook her head.

'That's right,' she said, tight-mouthed. 'And I reckon he never will again if Mr. Brett has his way. It could upset the little lad seeing him and learning who he is, after all this time.'

'He might be pleased to have his own father,' Rachel ventured, and once more Mrs. Handley gave a snort of derision.

'Best thing for that little mite is to let him stay just as he is,' she opined. 'He's had enough things happen to him in his little lifetime, bless him, he's best left alone with his uncle. There's nothing unstable about Mr. Brett, and the boy's not likely to have any more shocks while he has him.'

'Shocks?' Rachel looked puzzled, but she knew she was not destined to learn any more when she saw the tight, closed look on the housekeeper's face again.

'Talking's no good,' Mrs. Handley said. 'He's safe enough here with his uncle.'

It seemed to Rachel that past events at Seaways must have been even more disturbing than she had realised and she felt quite inextricably involved in them, even though she knew so little. Nicky's background was more unstable too than she had first feared and since her conversation with Mrs. Handley she felt a strong sense of protectiveness towards him.

It was three weeks since Lars had returned to Sweden and she was a little surprised to discover that she missed him rather less than she expected to. She missed his gallantry and his charm, of course, and it was always good for her morale that he was so obviously smitten, but Neil had spent much more time around the house during the past fortnight and he more than made up for his cousin's absence, though in a quite different way.

Neil spent more time with Nicky now, something that delighted Nicky and also threw Rachel into closer and more frequent contact with him. Since the appearance of Michael Browlett he seemed unwilling to let Nicky out of his sight for long and he had taken him riding several times. It was curious, but whenever she saw them together Rachel felt almost tearful, for their genuine affection for one another was quite touching and Nicky obviously enjoyed the extra attention he was receiving.

Rachel watched them approaching now, with Neil mounted on one of the geldings and toweringly tall beside Nicky perched astride the squat sturdiness of Taffy. Smiling to herself, she wondered at Neil's infinite patience with the boy's endless chatter as he urged Taffy to keep pace with his uncle's bigger mount.

She was much less nervous of the horses now that

she had become more used to them and after she had helped Nicky down she stood watching while his uncle made sure he took proper care of his mount. Young as he was Neil considered he was old enough to learn the correct way of doing things, and Rachel was bound to agree in principle. Neil, she thought, would make a strict but loving father and it was a pity he had no children of his own.

Hastily she pulled herself out of that realm of speculation and tried to concentrate on the activity that was going on in front of her. Thinking of Neil in that way was a fairly frequent occurrence lately, and the fact both disturbed and intrigued her. There was something about seeing him with Nicky that made him appear in quite a different light from the stern and autocratic landowner, and somehow she never tired of watching him or of being in his company.

With unsaddling and grooming completed Nicky raced off to offer Handley his help in unloading some newly arrived hay, and Rachel could hear him, chattering as always, giving the patient Handley his advice. She was about to follow Nicky across the yard to the feed-shed when Neil called out to her from the other end of the building.

'Rachel!'

She turned, her heart fluttering wildly as she looked at him. He was in the end stall completing the grooming of his own mount, and for a while she wondered if she had been mistaken in thinking she had heard him call her back, for he ceased his task only when she had walked the length of the stable and stood near him.

Then he straightened up, running one hand through the swathe of blond hair across his brow, his light blue eyes shadowed in the darkness of the stable, and her pulses stirred again when he looked at her. Fawn trousers fitted close to the strong muscular calves and his booted feet were planted firmly on the straw-covered floor. A thick cream wool sweater lent added darkness to his tanned and craggy features and he looked not only slightly aggressive but disturbingly and inescapably masculine.

As always Rachel's senses responded to him urgently and she did her best to still the deafening thud of her heart as she looked at him. 'You called me back,' she reminded him, and despaired to notice how unsteady her voice sounded.

A brief smile warmed Neil's blue eyes as he looked at her. 'I wondered if you knew that Lars was coming back in about ten days' time,' he said. 'I heard from him this morning.'

Rachel shook her head. 'No, I didn't,' she admitted, and wondered why he had taken the trouble to call her back when it would have been just as easy to mention it at lunch time. 'Nicky will be delighted,' she added, and Neil raised a brow curiously.

'I thought you would be,' he remarked, 'that's why I told you.' He half turned away for a moment, running a casual hand over the bay's glossy coat, not looking at her. 'Haven't you heard from him too?' he asked. 'I thought he would have told *you* he was coming.'

Rachel preferred not to think there was sarcasm intended and she shook her head slowly. 'I don't really see why he would,' she told him. 'Why should he keep me informed of his plans?'

Again Neil turned and looked at her directly, his blue eyes steady and glinting with challenge. 'Oh, don't be naïve, Rachel,' he said sharply. 'You know perfectly well why he'd let you know he was coming back—you're not so simple that you have to ask me that!'

His manner was both hurtful and unexpected, for during the past two weeks their former animosity had dwindled to almost nothing and she hated to see it return. 'And neither am I—whatever it is you think I am to Lars!' she told him in a voice that must have betrayed how she felt, and for a moment Neil simply looked at her steadily without saying anything.

Then he shook his head and there was a hint of smile on his lips as he half turned again, so that she could only see him in profile. 'You make it sound as if I accused you of something,' he told her, 'and nothing is further from the truth, Rachel. You know I have no interest at all in what you and Lars do, as long as it doesn't affect Nicky.'

'Of course—you've made that quite clear!' Rachel agreed shortly. It was hard to accept the fact of his disinterest without showing some resentment of it, and it was plain that her tone surprised him, for he raised a brow over it.

'I'd have to be quite blind, however,' he went on

coolly, 'not to realise that you—like him. Whenever you were together it was pretty obvious how you felt.'

Rachel had no idea why he had decided to stage this scene, but it was obvious that he meant to provoke her and she looked at him with bright, reproachful eyes, trying to see his reasons. She had never given him any cause to suppose that she took Lars' lighthearted romancing seriously and the present situation both puzzled and disturbed her.

'It—it would be silly to deny that I like Lars,' she told him in an unsteady voice. 'In fact I find him very attractive, any woman would, but I've known him for far too short a time for anyone to suggest there's anything serious about it, Neil! It's quite—quite ridiculous to suggest anything like that!'

His eyes were watching her again with an unnerving steadiness, focused on her mouth, as if it fascinated him, and Rachel could feel the rapid and uneven beat of her heart as it pounded uncontrollably. 'I merely suggested that you liked one another,' he reminded her gently, but Rachel shook her head.

'You only *said* that,' she insisted, 'but you implied a whole lot more, Neil, and it simply isn't true!'

Rachel's hands curled tightly into themselves when he shook his head slowly, his eyes shadowed and unfathomable. 'Shakespeare—I think it was Shakespeare,' he said quietly, 'who said—methinks the lady doth protest too much!'

'Neil!' There was no mistaking his meaning and she glared at him, both hurt and angry. 'You don't believe me!' she accused. 'Well, I—I don't care whether you do or not!'

'Why *should* you care?' Neil asked, and Rachel frowned.

She was trembling like a leaf, her eyes bright and glistening with what felt suspiciously like tears because she did not want to quarrel with Neil and he seemed bent on doing just that, though for what reason she could not imagine. She was alarmingly aware, as never before, of that powerful whipcord body standing so near, and the effect on her senses of a tangy combination of aftershave and leather, and there was nothing she could do about the tangle of sensations that made her head spin.

'Neil——' She hesitated, her eyes searching that strong rugged face for some clue to his reason for starting this. 'What are you trying to do?' she said in a small uncertain voice, and unbelievably he laughed and shook his head.

It was a soft deep sound that had the effect of making her heart beat so fast she instinctively put a hand to her breast. 'I'm not quite sure,' he confessed. 'But I know that Lars thinks he has only to raise his finger to you and you'll go to him—would you, Rachel?'

Rachel's heart clamoured so wildly that she had difficulty in breathing other than in short, uneven snatches, as if she had run a long way. 'No,' she whispered.

Somehow Neil's left hand was at her waist, its

broad palm spanning her slimness under her jacket, the fingers strong and irresistible as he drew her towards him. Then his right hand slid too beneath the thick wool jacket, bringing its strong persuasion to bear, pressing hard to the middle of her back until she was conscious of nothing but the powerful force of those steely arms, and the glittering brightness in his light blue eyes.

There was a sense of excitement in contact with his strong, hard and infinitely masculine body that shivered through her like fire and ice and she tried to say something, to murmur his name. But her voice came as no more than a faint whisper of sound which he smothered with his mouth before it became words.

Her arms reached up, encircling his neck, her hands in the thick blond hair above his ears, and her body was pressed so close to him that she was aware of every muscle straining her even closer. It was like nothing she had ever known before and she yielded to her own new and urgent needs with only a faint tremor of doubt.

Only once before had she been in his arms, when he had rescued her from that icy ledge above the sea, and she had found comfort there then. Now there was a sensuous, irresistible excitement that demanded a response from her—a response that she gave willingly enough.

'Neil! Miss Carson!'

The childish treble penetrated Rachel's mind only dimly at first, but then Neil released her, reluctantly she felt, and stood looking down at her.

His hands were still at her waist, hard and warm through her sweater, and his eyes, shadowed in the semi-darkness, gleamed as warmly as ever.

There was a hint of smile on his mouth, a smile that somehow disturbed her, and he inclined his head towards the open door into the yard where Nicky's insistent shrill voice was calling to them again. 'I think someone had better go and rescue Handley,' he said, and for a moment Rachel looked up at him uncertainly.

'Neil! Miss Carson!'

Nicky's voice came nearer as he ran across the yard, and Rachel stepped back suddenly, turning towards the door, her eyes slightly dazed still. Her heart was beating with such violence that it was difficult to think clearly, but it was obvious that Neil was perfectly controlled and somehow that troubled her.

The faint smile still crooked one corner of his mouth and his eyes seemed, to Rachel's sensitive gaze, to hold a hint of mockery for those few heart-stopping seconds that had affected her so deeply. She looked at him steadily, almost appealingly, for several seconds and she thought she saw a change in his expression, but then Nicky came hurtling in at the door, his voice shrilly indignant.

'You didn't answer me!' he accused. 'Why didn't you answer me?' He stopped for a moment, standing in front of them, and there was a small frown between his brows, then he took Rachel's hand and tugged at it. 'I'm hungry,' he declared. 'I'm hungry, Miss Carson!'

It was Neil who answered him, pulling off his riding cap and ruffling his thick hair into tumbled untidiness. 'You're always hungry,' he told him with a smile. 'And it's no use worrying Miss Carson about it, because it isn't time for your lunch yet.'

'But she promised me chocolate,' Nicky declared indignantly, and Neil glanced at her curiously.

'Did you do that?' he asked.

Rachel nodded. 'Yes, I'm afraid I did.'

There was a curious glint in Neil's eyes as he looked at her for a moment without speaking, his hand still on Nicky's untidy head. 'Do you often indulge him with chocolate?' he asked.

Still trembling from his kiss, Rachel found it hard to give her mind to more mundane things, but she glanced down at Nicky's anxious and faintly indignant face before she replied. 'I—I do sometimes,' she said. 'Not very often.' She felt that the glitter in his eyes betrayed disapproval and almost unconsciously her chin thrust out in a brief gesture of defiance. 'I *thought* you wouldn't approve!' she said.

'But you still did it?'

The softness of his voice shivered over her like ice and she clung to Nicky's small hand tightly. 'Only occasionally,' she insisted. Somehow his easy transition to stern guardian angered her because he could so easily shrug off that soul-stirring incident of a moment ago when she still trembled from its effect. Looking down at Nicky, she pulled a rueful face. 'You'd better not have your chocolate, Nicky,' she told him. 'Your uncle doesn't want you to

133

have it—I'm sorry.'

Nicky looked up at his uncle with his lower lip quivering suspiciously, almost ready to cry, and his huge eyes were wide and accusing. 'But, Neil——' he began.

'Of course you can have it,' Neil told him quietly. 'You were promised it and I don't believe in breaking promises.' Without a word Rachel reached into her jacket pocket and handed Nicky the promised chocolate, her cheeks flushed as she suffered Neil's steady gaze. He gave the boy time to remove the wrappings then ruffled his hair encouragingly. 'You go and watch Handley for a minute,' he told him. 'Miss Carson won't be long.'

Nicky, munching happily on his treat, went out into the yard again and the sound of his voice when he called out to Handley in the feed-shed came back to them clearly on the cold air. Uncertain why she was being detained, Rachel made a tentative move to follow him, but a large hand thudded firmly on to the wooden partition beside her and startled her into pressing herself back against it.

An arm barred her way, a strong muscular arm that she knew from experience would be quite capable of stopping her by force if necessary, and she felt trapped. The vigorous arrogance of his stance set her pulses racing and she turned her head away swiftly when he leaned on his hand, a movement that brought his face close to hers and the sensual warmth of his body into contact with her own trembling form.

'Now,' Neil said firmly, 'perhaps you'll be good

enough to explain the reason for that little scene just now. Why you told Nicky I wouldn't let him have his chocolate.'

'I didn't,' Rachel denied breathlessly. 'I only——'

'I'm not an idiot and neither am I deaf, Rachel!' He leaned closer, pressing her lightly against the partition, and his other hand gripped her chin suddenly, turning her to face him and making her gasp at the strength of his fingers. 'I don't like being made to appear the ogre you made me,' he told her, 'and especially not to Nicky!'

'Neil, please, I didn't *mean* anything by it,' she insisted. 'I—I just said it because—because I was angry.'

'Angry?' The relentless fingers kept her facing him and she bit her lip anxiously, shivering when his breath warmed her mouth. 'Why?' he asked softly. 'Why were you angry? Was it because I kissed you?'

Her heart racing wildly she shook her head. 'How could it be that?' she whispered huskily. 'That wasn't anything important, was it, Neil?'

'Rachel!'

Her legs felt so weak that she could barely stand and the rapid throb of the pulse in her temple almost stifled her as she stood there, her body just touched by the vigorous, masculine warmth of his. It was the heavy clump of Handley's boots on the yard outside that snatched her back from a kind of haze of unreality.

'Nicky,' she said breathlessly. 'I can't hear him, Neil, he—he must have gone!'

'It doesn't matter, he won't go far!' The strong firm arm still blocked her way and his eyes gleamed with determination despite Handley's nearness.

'But I must go after him!' Rachel insisted, and ducked swiftly under his arm. The move caught him by surprise and she managed to run the length of the stable before he caught up with her. His fingers curled round her arm, stopping her short, and he would have swung her round again to face him, but Handley's curious gaze was on them and Rachel took advantage of Neil's hesitation to shake herself free. 'It was *your* instructions that Nicky mustn't be left alone,' she reminded him in a husky whisper. 'He's on his way back to the house, but I can catch up with him if I hurry!'

For a moment she thought he was going to argue with her despite Handley's interested proximity, but then he let her go suddenly and shrugged his shoulders resignedly. Rachel turned and ran after Nicky and her heart was thudding hard in her breast as she caught up with him. She had an almost irresistible urge to turn round and see if Neil was watching, but instead she put a hand on Nicky's head and smiled as they walked down the bridle path to the house.

With Lars being back it meant that both Rachel and Nicky would inevitably see less of Neil, for Lars was almost sure to take over some of what Rachel referred to as the bodyguard duties. She was unsure just how she felt about having Lars taking Neil's place, but it was a fact that she found Lars a much less disturbing companion.

There had been snow during the day and now, as the evening drew on, there was a crispness in the air that promised frost by morning, and the stars were clear and bright around the fat yellow winter moon. Nicky was in bed and Rachel had succumbed to Lars' persuasion to come for a stroll as far as the gates, looking up at the stars where they appeared between the tangle of skeleton branches overhead.

It was vaguely creepy walking down the drive at night with their own shadows drifting silently beside them and, quite involuntarily, she shivered. 'Are you cold?' Lars was immediately concerned for her, putting an arm round her shoulders, his fingers strong and comforting on her arm. 'Is that better?' he asked, and Rachel smiled.

There was something disarmingly frank about Lars that was almost irresistible. 'I'm not really cold,' she told him. 'It was just someone walking over my grave, that's all.'

They walked in silence for a while and somewhere an owl wooed the full moon with its soft call, the bare trees shivering in the wind that brought colour to Rachel's cheeks and made her glad of Lars' additional warmth about her shoulders. The thin layer of snow on the drive already crackled faintly when they trod on it and confirmed the early signs of frost. In a way there was a strange, gaunt beauty about winter that Rachel had never discovered in town and, once she had walked long enough to stimulate her circulation, she felt quite glowingly warm.

'What have you been doing with yourself while I've been away?' Lars asked, and she smiled up at him, shaking her head.

'Nothing out of the ordinary,' she told him. 'Of course it's made a difference not being allowed to take Nicky very far afield, but——' She paused, wondering if he yet knew about Michael Browlett's unexpected appearance. There had been little enough time to mention it since his arrival that afternoon, but it was possible that Neil saw the incident as important enough to mention. 'Do—did Neil tell you about Nicky's father?' she ventured, and Lars nodded.

'He told me,' he said, 'but I can't help feeling that he's taking the whole thing too seriously.'

'Perhaps.' She was unwilling to pass judgment on Neil because she had no doubt at all that he cared deeply for his little nephew and would never consider anything that concerned his well-being as too much trouble to take seriously. 'I didn't realise who the man was,' Rachel told him. 'Not until Neil told me, he recognised his description. It's odd,' she mused, frowning curiously, 'but he asked me to identify Neil—doesn't he know him? And how could Neil recognise *him*?'

'Lynn had a photograph, I believe,' Lars told her, 'but I never saw it, and he never came to Seaways, of course.'

'Of course?' She echoed the words curiously. 'Why was that, Lars? Didn't the family accept him?'

Lars shrugged, the moonlight revealing a new ruggedness in his good-looking features that gave him the same suggestion of strength his cousin had. 'No one saw him,' he told her. 'Lynn eloped with him, and when she was expecting Nicky—he left her. I doubt if Lynn herself knew him for more than a few months.'

It was not at all as Rachel had imagined it, despite Mrs. Handley's moment of confidence, and she said nothing for a few moments, trying yet again to find some kind of stability in Nicky's early background. The wonder was that he was as normal and friendly a child as he was with the bad start he had had in life.

'But why?' she asked, and went on to explain when she saw Lars' puzzled frown. 'I mean, Lynn came from a wealthy family, if he was a—a fortune-hunter, which I assume is what the family think, surely it made little difference to his position whether they had a child or not—his wife was still rich.'

'Oh, Lynn was wealthy,' Lars agreed, 'but Mrs. Fran Munger was—still is—even wealthier, and Michael Browlett caught her eye. He was working in the States, only playing small parts, but not so small he was overlooked by one of the richest women in the world.'

'He's an actor?' Rachel asked. 'I didn't know that.'

'He hasn't needed to do much for the past five years,' Lars told her dryly. 'He's been living the life of Riley in America.'

'And now he's back in England,' Rachel mused. 'I wonder why.'

Lars' arm tightened around her shoulders and he laughed shortly, his face half buried in her hair. 'You don't keep up with the interational gossip columns, it's obvious, Rachel,' he said. 'Mrs. Fran Munger married another husband last month, another millionaire, of course—Michael Browlett's lost his meal ticket!'

CHAPTER EIGHT

It was a fairly warm day with a promise of sun behind the thick damp mist that presently hung over the countryside and gave only glimpses of distance, making Rachel feel that Seaways was isolated in a soft grey cloud, miles from anywhere. It was a curious feeling and she shivered a little as she dressed, again reminded of that hint of mystery that seemed always to be present in the old house.

While she stood brushing her hair in front of the mirror her mind again returned to Michael Browlett, Nicky's father, and she wondered if he really would try to gain control of his son now that he needed him for the fortune he would bring with him. Surely, she thought, no court would uphold the claim of a father who had never seen nor attempted to see his son until his own financial straits made him realise what a desirable acquisition he would be.

And Neil—what of Neil, if his brother-in-law's claim were to be successful? Losing Nicky would break his heart, and she could not bear to think of it happening. While she was supervising Nicky's toilet she realised, too, how much a change of guardianship would affect her. Not only because she had become very attached to Nicky over the past couple of months, but because if Nicky was no longer at Seaways she would no longer be needed there herself, and that was a prospect she faced very unwillingly, even though it was bound to happen sooner or later when Nicky got older.

Ready at last, she walked down the stairs behind Nicky's small, hurrying figure, and wondered for the first time just what she would do when her time at Seaways was finished. Her training had taught her that it was inadvisable to become too attached either to her charge or her environment, but somehow she felt so inextricably part of Seaways and the family who lived there that the idea of leaving dismayed her. Not the least disturbing part was the prospect of never seeing Neil again once she had outlived her usefulness to him.

Nicky burst into the breakfast room with his usual bright good morning for his uncle, and he had wriggled himself up on to his chair before Rachel even had time to enter the room. It was a surprise to find Neil alone, for usually by the time she and Nicky came down for their breakfasts Neil and Lars had almost finished theirs, but this morning Neil had barely begun.

Raising a brow, Neil looked first at his wristwatch and then at the clock on the mantel, as if he doubted their accuracy. 'Good morning,' he said, and a faint smile tugged at one corner of his wide mouth when he looked at her. 'You've beaten Lars to it today, you're early.'

Rachel finished tucking a serviette under Nicky's chin before she looked at her own wristwatch and then she too glanced at the mantel clock and frowned. 'My watch is very fast,' she mused, 'I'd no idea we were so early.' She looked across at Neil and half smiled. 'I hope we shan't disturb your peace too much if we join you.'

He shook his head and she caught a bright quizzical look in the blue eyes that regarded her from below the thick sweep of blond hair across his brow. 'Not at all,' he told her, 'as long as you're not disappointed because Lars isn't here too.'

Rachel, suspecting his motives, looked across at him and frowned. 'Of course not,' she denied quietly. 'Why should we be? Lars will be down soon enough, I expect.'

'Sure to be,' Neil agreed. 'He'll be taking Nicky riding, won't he?' He ate in silence for a moment while Rachel saw to it that Nicky had a bowl of cereal to appease his appetite. 'I'm surprised Lars hasn't taught you to ride,' Neil observed after a few seconds. 'Then you could go with him and Nicky.'

As it was something that had crossed her own mind more than once as a possibility Rachel looked across at him briefly and shook her head. 'I had thought about it,' she confessed, 'but then I remembered that you wouldn't agree to it.'

Neil flicked one light brow swiftly upwards and the blue eyes held hers steadily for as long as she could bear the scrutiny. 'Oh?' he queried. 'What gave you that idea?'

'For one thing,' Rachel told him a little uncertainly, 'because they're your horses and you'd be paying me while I was learning.'

Neil ate in silence for several seconds, then he

looked directly across at her in the same moment that she glanced up, and colour flooded warmly into her cheeks when she met his eyes, her heart thudding hard at her ribs. 'You still have a bad opinion of me, don't you, Rachel?' he asked in a soft voice. 'Do you really see me as such an ogre that I'd forbid you to learn to ride just because you work for me? Is that how you see me—as some kind of martinet?'

'Oh no, of course I don't!' She was uncomfortably aware that Nicky was beginning to take an interest in what they were saying and it almost changed her mind about reminding Neil about her first meeting with him. Then glancing at Nicky from the corner of her eye she looked directly at Neil. 'But you did say before I started work for you,' she reminded him, 'that you didn't see why you should pay me to learn!'

It was touch and go, she realised breathlessly, whether or not he lost his temper, and she could feel her heart hammering with such violence at her ribs that it made her head spin. Then he smiled, a tight, bitter smile that showed in his eyes as an icy glitter. 'I asked you, if I remember,' he said coolly, 'if you expected me to pay you to gain experience.' Briefly the blue eyes held hers determinedly and she shivered involuntarily. 'I should have known you'd remember that,' he said, and Rachel flushed.

'I'm—I'm sorry.' She half whispered the words and was aware that not only Neil's blue eyes were watching her but Nicky's too, and she shook her head anxiously as she took up her own cereal spoon and began to eat. 'I shouldn't have mentioned it,' she admitted, and Neil laughed shortly.

'But you couldn't resist it!' He eyed her quizzically for a second or two, then leaned forward on one elbow. 'I suppose Lars knows your reason for not learning to ride?' he suggested, and she shook her head. 'Didn't you tell him it was because of what I'd say that you couldn't learn?'

'The question of my learning to ride has never arisen,' Rachel informed him a little breathlessly. 'Lars has never mentioned it and I'm not sure whether I'd like it or not, although it would be nice to be able to go out with Nicky and Lars.'

'And with me?' Neil suggested quietly.

Rachel could feel the hand holding her spoon trembling like a leaf and she hastily put down the spoon and clasped her two hands together while she looked across at him warily. 'If you asked me to,' she told him in a small breathless voice, and he half smiled, his eyes searching her face, lingering on her mouth in that disturbing, intense way that set her pulses racing.

'I'm driving into Mergeton this morning,' he said quietly. 'If you——' He stopped in mid-sentence when the door of the breakfast room opened and Lars came in.

Nicky shouted a greeting and started immediately asking about their ride after breakfast, and Rachel murmured a greeting as she hastily picked up her spoon again, conscious that Lars was frowning over the bright flush in her cheeks. It was several seconds before quiet descended again and

Rachel suddenly realised that Neil had already finished his breakfast and was drinking down the last of his coffee without bothering with toast and marmalade.

He got to his feet murmuring an apology and ruffling one big hand in Nicky's thick brown hair as he passed him. 'Be good,' he admonished him, and strode towards the door. He did not, Rachel noticed, even glance again in her direction and she felt strangely bereft as the door closed behind him and his tall, lean shape disappeared into the hall.

She would have given much to know what he had started to say to her when Lars appeared. From the little she had heard she felt almost sure it had been an invitation to drive into Mergeton with him and she knew she would have accepted without question if Lars had not interrupted. What she found harder to face was the apparently easy way he had given up the idea when his cousin appeared, and she wondered if he still believed her to be more than half in love with Lars.

It was pleasant having Lars back again at Seaways, but after the past weeks Rachel was ready to admit that she missed Neil's company much more even than she had expected to. Sometimes it was difficult to understand her own feelings where Neil was concerned and she had long since accepted the fact that he could affect her emotionally much more deeply than Lars or anyone else ever could.

As for the strange love–hate relationship that Lars and Neil had, it was past her understanding, although it possibly had something to do with the fact that blood was thicker than water, and they reminded her more of brothers sometimes than cousins. They could disagree as violently as Rachel had heard them do and yet there was no suggestion that Lars should stay away from Seaways for good. Even his affair with Lynn had not brought that about.

During the past few days, since Lars' return, the weather had taken a definite turn for the better and it almost seemed there was a touch of spring in the air, although early morning saw wet, chill mists rolling in from the sea over the farmlands.

Things were more or less as before, with Nicky riding every day with Lars and the three of them taking a walk sometimes. Rachel said nothing about Neil's near-invitation to drive with him into Mergeton, if that was what he had intended, and she hoped Nicky would have forgotten about it too, for Lars would find it too much not to comment on it and she felt oddly shy about it.

Obviously Nicky would have gone with them and yet, somewhere in the back of her mind, was the odd feeling of certainty that he had meant the invitation for her alone, and she could not shake off the sense of excitement it gave her. More difficult to understand and to accept was the way he had suddenly cut short the invitation.

'We could drive into Mergeton again,' Lars suggested, and Rachel nodded agreement without really hearing what he said.

'But not today,' Lars qualified hastily when

Nicky showed signs of demanding immediate departure. 'I'd like to make it a whole day's outing, and we've already lost half of today.'

'Tomorrow?' Nicky demanded, anxious to have the matter settled as soon as possible, and Lars smiled down at him tolerantly.

'Maybe, little one,' he told him. 'If Rachel would like to.'

He ostensibly gave an answer to Nicky, but he looked at Rachel as he made it and it was obvious that her preoccupation puzzled him to some extent. Neil would have no objection, of course, to them going into Mergeton with Lars and all of them would enjoy the change. Although it had almost certainly not been Neil's intention to confine them, his edict that they should not go far afield without either himself or Handley in attendance had done just that in effect. Reluctant to trouble them very often, when both men had work to do, their movements had been restricted whether Neil meant it so or not, by her unwillingness to ask.

'I'd like that,' she told Lars. 'It'll make a change to go out for the day.'

Lars' blue eyes glistened with laughter, not altogether without malice, Rachel thought, and he looked down at her with one fair brow raised. 'Hasn't Neil taken you anywhere?' he asked, and Rachel shook her head.

'It isn't any part of Neil's job to take me out,' she told Lars defensively, perhaps more defensively than she realised, for she saw Lars' good-looking face register surprise at her tone. 'He's very busy always and I'm quite capable of going into Merge-ton alone in my time off. If I'd wanted to take Nicky anywhere I'm sure he'd have taken us if I'd asked him, but as it happened we were quite happy here.'

Lars once more flicked a brow into the thick fair hair over his forehead and his blue eyes regarded her speculatively. 'So you're Neil's champion now,' he remarked. 'I find that rather a surprise, Rachel, I always thought you and Neil were——' One expressive hand conveyed with remarkable explicitness her initial antagonism towards Neil and she found herself unable to resist a smile, although her cheeks burned pinkly under that speculating scrutiny. Nicky was running ahead of them and she was thankful he was not near enough to overhear them.

'I'm no one's champion, Lars,' she told him in a quiet and studiously controlled voice. 'I merely stated a fact—Neil's under no obligation at all to take *me* out, and if I want to take Nicky anywhere it's up to me to ask him to take us.'

Lars blue eyes teased her and he slid an arm around her shoulders, drawing her close to him so that she was conscious of the warm vibrance of his body. 'Nor am I under any obligation,' he told her, 'but I want to take you out for my own pleasure—I would have thought Neil was as capable of appreciating that fact as much as I do!'

'Neil's my employer,' Rachel reminded him, looking up at him and smiling, 'you're not!'

'And therefore better placed for taking advantage of you,' Lars pointed out with embarrassing frankness, and smiled at her broadly. 'As I would do!'

With the memory of Neil's kiss all too easily brought to mind, Rachel shrugged uneasily. 'Maybe,' she said.

'For instance,' Lars went on undeterred, 'in his place I'd have taken you with me into Mergeton today, even if it is on business and even if it meant taking Nicky along too.'

It was tempting to tell him how close she had come to being asked to go with Neil, but Rachel resisted it, for she was not yet ready to face Lars' speculation once he knew about it. 'I'd hardly expect him to take passengers when he's on a business trip,' she told him, and Lars laughed and hugged her to him again.

'Oh well,' he said, 'his loss is my gain!' He dropped a light kiss on her cheek. 'While Neil sorts out Nicky's financial affairs, I go walking with you—I think I have the advantage of him!'

'*Nicky's* financial affairs?'

Rachel looked at him curiously. It had never occurred to her that Nicky might be wealthy in his own right and she had to do some rapid readjustment. She had seen him only as a poor orphan, and assumed that he had nothing of his own, whereas a child in his position, of course, was quite likely to have money of his own.

His mother had in all probability been as wealthy as his uncle was and almost certainly Nicky would have been her heir. Neil, naturally, being his guardian, would assume responsibility for his financial affairs as well, so his business trip was quite understandable.

Lars was looking at her curiously, as if he half suspected her innocence in the matter was assumed. 'Didn't you realise how rich Nicky is in his own right?' he asked, and Rachel shook her head.

'It hadn't even occurred to me,' she confessed. 'I simply thought that Neil took care of him because no one else would. It never occurred to me that he was a—a poor little rich boy.'

'I suppose that's what he is,' Lars agreed thoughtfully. 'Although he's likely to be even richer, the way Neil handles his investments, and he's much happier now Neil has sole charge of him than he ever was with Lynn.'

Another fragment, Rachel thought musingly, another indication that neither Nicky nor his mother had led very happy or secure lives. 'I see,' was all she said, and asked no more questions. Neil seemed to loom so large in everyone's life that she wondered what they would all have done without him.

She walked beside Lars, thoughtfully quiet, for some time, and the fresh wind whipped colour into her cheeks and blew the soft wisps of dark hair back from her forehead where it peeped from beneath the woollen hat she wore. Watching Nicky playing just ahead of them she pondered on how much else there was to learn about Nicky and his mother. Lynn became more of a mystery all the time and she was more than ever convinced that the worst was yet to come.

Nicky was happy—happier than he had ever been, if Lars and Mrs. Handley were to be believed, and she wondered if Lars would ever have had the courage or the inclination to care for him as Neil did. She thought not. She was aware suddenly that Lars was looking down at her and he smiled when she looked up at him enquiringly.

'Shall we?' he asked, and indicated a low brick wall that flanked the steps up to the front door. When she nodded he drew her across to it and sat himself down, pulling her down beside him and placing an arm around her waist. 'Why do you think Michael Browlett is suddenly taking an interest in his son?' he asked, and Rachel shook her head.

They sat looking across at the damp, untidy shrubbery with its cheerless winter tangle given a brief beauty by the pale sun shining on wet leaves and bare branches. Somewhere near Nicky was making his favourite engine noises as he ran in and out of the trees and shrubs, much too energetic to sit down.

'You mean——' Rachel looked up at Lars uneasily. It was hard to attribute such callousness to anyone connected with Nicky, but the fact had to be faced.

'He has to find a way of earning a living again now,' Lars reminded her bluntly, and Rachel shook her head slowly.

'That—that simply hadn't occurred to me,' she

said after a moment or two. 'But I suppose it's possible that he would do something like that. If he could get custody of Nicky——'

'He'd be in charge of a goldmine,' Lars assured her wryly. 'Neil's done well investing Nicky's money.'

'But only for Nicky's sake!' Rachel insisted hastily. 'He wouldn't do anything wrong, not with Nicky's money, not Neil!'

'Not Neil,' Lars echoed, and turned her until she was half facing him, his blue eyes searching her face, a dark speculative look in their depths. Sooner or later, she knew, Lars would again remark about her frequent defence of Neil, but her reactions were purely instinctive and there seemed little she could do about it.

Her heart was thudding hard at her ribs and she could feel its urgency even through the thick jacket she wore, where her hands pressed together in the pockets in front of her. There was a bright flush in her cheeks too that was not entirely due to the brisk wind and Lars' blue gaze missed nothing of it.

It was strange, but being so close to Lars was much less exciting than the same proximity would have been with Neil, and she dared not stop to wonder why. Lars was young and good-looking and she was definitely attracted to him, but somehow he simply did not have the same profound effect on her senses that Neil did.

He put a finger under her chin and gently lifted her face to him and his eyes were fixed on her mouth. His voice, much too soft for Nicky to hear even if he had been nearer, was warm and persuasive and so very faintly accented that it was barely discernible. 'You're very lovely, Rachel,' he said. 'Much too lovely to be buried here at Seaways.'

'But I'm not buried,' Rachel denied hastily. 'I love it here, Lars, you know that.'

'And I love you!' He made the statement firmly and confidently, despite the softness of his voice, but it was scarcely credible that he meant it and Rachel stared at him unbelievingly.

His breath was warm on her lips and she felt her heart beating urgently as she tried to turn her head away, to avoid that steady gaze that fixed itself on her mouth so unwaveringly. But Lars was not to be denied and he substituted a large but gentle hand for the one finger that supported her chin and made movement impossible.

'Lars.' She tried to keep her voice steady, but it trembled in spite of her efforts and she licked her lips anxiously. 'You've—it's only a little over three weeks that you've known me, Lars,' she pointed out. 'It—it isn't very long.'

'But it's long enough,' Lars assured her close to her mouth. 'You mustn't expect me to waste time as Neil does, sweetheart. He had you to himself for several weeks, but he has not taken advantage of his opportunities—I will!'

'No, Lars!' She managed at last to free herself of that persistent hand on her chin and looked at him with bright, anxious eyes. 'I—I like you,' she admitted. 'In fact I find you very attractive, if you prefer me to be frank, but I'm—I can't let myself be swept along like this as if I have no say in the matter.'

'Oh, but of course you do,' Lars assured her earnestly. 'I am hoping that you love me too—that would make everything right.'

'I—I don't.' She looked at him in dismay, so afraid of being swept up into something she could not control. 'I've said I—I like you, but that's all, Lars. I don't love you.'

Lars' blue eyes were warm and persuasive and he held her in the curve of his arm, hugged close to him, his mouth only inches away. 'I could persuade you,' he said softly. 'I want you to come back to Sweden with me when I go next time. Will you do that, Rachel?'

Rachel stared at him, shaking her head slowly when she recalled her conversation with Neil in the stable. 'Lars thinks he has only to raise his finger and you'll go,' Neil had told her, and she had denied it. Now she was faced with an invitation that it was obvious Lars fully expected her to accept, unless she had taken it all more seriously than he intended.

'Don't be silly,' she said in a small husky voice, 'of course I can't come to Sweden with you!'

'I see nothing to stop you,' Lars insisted coolly. 'You will surely not be expected to work for a whole year without a holiday, and once I have you to myself I'm sure I can persuade you to feel differently about me! Let me try, hmm?'

'Oh, Lars, please be sensible!' She looked at him wide-eyed, not sure, even yet, that he could be completely serious. 'I haven't known you nearly long enough to—to just go traipsing off to Sweden with you!'

'You'd rather stay with Neil?'

He asked the question quietly, but Rachel detected the edge of steel in his voice and shook her head slowly. The innuendo was unmistakable and it touched on a very delicate nerve, but she was not prepared to admit to Lars that she would prefer to stay with Neil, if it came to a choice.

'I'd rather stay in a very good job,' she told him, and hoped she sounded as firm and cool as she tried to. 'I've no one to compare him with, I know, because this is my first post, but Neil's a very good employer and I'm very happy at Seaways.'

'But even Neil cannot dictate where you spend your holidays,' Lars insisted. 'And I'm sure I could persuade you round to my way once I had you to myself.'

Rachel looked up at him for a moment steadily. This, she thought, must be what Neil had been warning him about when she had heard them quarrelling so bitterly that morning. He had warned Lars not to involve her and Lars had retorted that she, Rachel, was not Lynn. For the first time she wondered if he had ever put the same proposition to Lynn and if Lynn had been easier to persuade into going off to Sweden than she was herself.

'I couldn't do it, Lars,' she said. 'For one thing

Neil would know it wasn't simply a—a holiday.' She shook her head firmly. 'No, Lars, I couldn't.'

'I don't see how it concerns Neil,' Lars insisted, his blue eyes resenting her refusal, while one hand stroked the side of her face that was turned to him. 'You'd know it was something more than a holiday, and so would I, but whether Neil knew or not isn't important. If you want to come there's nothing he could do about it!'

Rachel eased away from the caressing hand that stroked her cheek and shook her head, brushing back the wisps of hair from her face. 'He wouldn't care one way or the other what I did,' she told Lars, and looked up sharply when he laughed, her brows drawn into a frown.

'Oh, he'd care,' Lars said confidently. 'He'd certainly care!'

For a moment Rachel looked at him, her eyes searching his good-looking face for a clue as to his meaning, and her heart was thudding anxiously as she sat huddled on the low wall, her hands in her pockets, curled tightly. 'Enough to decide I wasn't fit to look after Nicky any longer maybe,' she said, far more matter-of-factly than she felt. 'And I couldn't blame him for that, Lars.'

'Rachel!' He reached out and stroked her cheek again, his eyes glowing warmly as he looked down at her, so persuasive and confident he was hard to resist.

She pushed aside his hand, quite gently, and held his gaze for as long as she was able, then looked down at the firm, confident smile on his mouth and shook her head. 'I won't be persuaded, Lars,' she told him, and looked down at her wrist-watch, 'and I think it's time we went in now, it's getting colder and Nicky——'

It was quiet, she realised suddenly, much too quiet if Nicky was still pretending to be an aircraft and making those noisy engine sounds he was so fond of. The only thing she could hear was the soft rustle of the wind in the shrubbery and somewhere in the distance the sound of a car, gradually disappearing along the road.

'Nicky!' She got to her feet, her hands and legs trembling, straining to hear the slightest sound of that mock aeroplane. He never ignored a call, not more than once, and she called again. 'Nicky!' It was quiet—too quiet.

Lars, jerked into action by the edge of panic on her voice, got to his feet and strode across to where the wet, sad-looking shrubs huddled under the bare trees, and there was a note of anxiety in his voice too when he called, 'Nicky!'

CHAPTER NINE

IT was little more than an hour and a half since it happened, but to Rachel it seemed like hours since she had suddenly decided to call Nicky to her and go inside. Since she had got up from her seat on the wall to call him and received no reply. Her eyes were dark with anxiety and hazy with unshed tears as she stared blankly in a kind of stunned disbelief at Lars.

Lars too showed the effects of shock on his good-looking face as he stood facing her in the hall, neither of them daring to suggest what had really happened. He looked pale and drawn and it was difficult to believe he was the same man she had sat with only a short time ago, a man so full of self-confidence and brimming with ideas for taking her to Sweden with him.

The laughter and the air of confidence were gone and he ran one hand through his thick blond hair in a gesture of despair—a gesture that reminded her of Neil. It was the reminder of Neil that made Rachel sick with apprehension, for the thought of having to break the news to him dismayed her almost more than the actual fact of Nicky's disappearance.

It was a fact now that had to be faced—Nicky *had* disappeared and no amount of self-delusion would make any difference. It had seemed like no more than a few minutes that she and Lars had sat on the wall beside the steps discussing the rights and wrongs of her going back to Sweden with him and whether or not Rachel could ever love him, but in that short time they were preoccupied with their own affairs they had not even noticed that Nicky's familiar engine noises were no longer audible.

It was only when they called to him and he did not reply that the awful truth began to dawn on them—he was no longer within calling distance, he was no longer anywhere at all that she could see, and Rachel's heart had almost stopped when she realised what had happened.

The worst part was realising that she had done exactly what Neil had been so insistent on avoiding. She had become so involved in her conversation with Lars that Nicky had been left to play alone and out of sight. Neil would never forgive her, and that would be the hardest fact to face—the knowledge that she had betrayed his trust in her.

At first she and Lars had searched for him, only half believing he was actually missing and still hoping that he was hiding somewhere, that even if he had gone off alone he could not have gone very far. But eventually they had been forced to face the fact that it was not simply a game and Mr. and Mrs. Handley had been enlisted to help look for him, though with no more success. It was clearly that wherever Nicky was he was nowhere at Seaways, and someone was going to have to break it to Neil when he came home.

The sound of his car on the drive immediately put her into a state of near-panic and Rachel looked up at Lars with anxious grey eyes, her mouth trembling. He was going to be not only angry but hurt and she could see only herself as the culprit at the moment.

'I—I can't,' she whispered huskily. 'I—I don't know how I'm going to tell him, Lars!'

Suddenly it seemed Lars looked much older and there were lines that ran from his mouth and betrayed an anxiety at least as great as her own, but he put a firm and comforting hand on her shoulder when he spoke. 'Leave it to me,' he told her. 'I'll tell him, Rachel.' His accent, she noticed absently, was much more pronounced than ever before, and she wondered if he too felt panic at the idea of breaking the news to his cousin.

She shook her head, still seeing herself as the culprit, and tears trembled on her lashes as she stood listening to Neil's firm, confident tread on the steps. She put up her hands to her mouth to check the anguish that caught in her throat and threatened to choke her. 'No,' she whispered. 'I—I have to, Lars; it's—Nicky was was my responsibility!'

There was no time for Lars to argue whose responsibility it was, because Neil was already coming in through the door, a tall forceful figure in the more formal dress he had put on for his visit to town—dark grey tweed that somehow made him look even bigger than usual and a cream shirt that

161

showed off the tanned ruggedness of his features.

He glanced only briefly at Lars, then swept immediately round to Rachel's pale tearful face, his eyes narrowed. 'What's happened?' he asked in a flat, almost resigned voice that was somehow more affecting than an outburst of anger would have been. 'In God's name, Rachel, what's happened?'

'Nicky——' Her voice choked in her throat and the tears she had tried so hard to contain flooded down her cheeks when she saw the blank stunned look in his eyes. 'It—it's Nicky,' she tried again, 'he——' Again her voice and her courage failed her and she simply shook her head.

'Tell me!' Strong hands gripped her shoulders so hard that she cried out and her head spun dizzily when he shook her. 'Where's Nicky?' he rasped harshly. 'Where is he, Rachel? What's happened to him?'

'He's gone—he's missing, Neil!' It was Lars who answered for her and Neil swung round on him, his blue eyes hard and icy and his mouth set relentlessly while strong fingers still dug hard into Rachel's shoulders.

'How?' he demanded. 'How could he go missing when you and Rachel were with him?' Lars cast a brief, telling glance at Rachel, saying no word but telling Neil all he needed to know, and his eyes narrowed until they were little more than icy slits. 'Yes, of course,' he said, his voice steely hard, 'you had other things on your mind, didn't you?'

'Neil, please!' Rachel cried in despair. 'It—it wasn't how you make it sound at all, please——'

'It doesn't matter a damn *how* it sounds!' Neil interrupted harshly. 'The only thing that matters to me is finding Nicky. I presume you've searched the grounds and the house thoroughly; have you informed the police?'

Rachel stared at him, too stunned to reply, and it was Lars who once again answered for her, following the meaning all too easily, apparently, for he looked at Neil warily. 'Do you think we should?' he asked. 'If Nicky's only——'

'Do you think he's only?' Neil asked coldly, and Lars shook his head. 'It's obvious who Nicky's with, and the sooner we can have him stopped the better.'

'Oh, no!'

Rachel put her hands to her mouth and stared at him over trembling fingers, her eyes wide and unbelieving. Neil looked at her for a moment with that same steady, ice-cold gaze that made her shiver miserably, and his mouth betrayed the derision he felt for her reaction. 'You don't approve of having the police informed?' he asked harshly. 'Perhaps you have a better idea of how to get Nicky back?'

'I—I don't have an idea at all,' Rachel admitted miserably. 'But if he's with——'

'Oh, he's with his father,' Neil assured her in a cold, flat voice, 'I've no doubt about that at all. Is that what you wanted, Rachel? Has your training taught you that there's no substitute for the natural parent, no matter how callous or uncaring he might be? Is that what they taught you?'

It was almost as if he had struck her a physical

blow and Rachel closed her eyes for a second on the hard and pitiless look in his eyes. She was shivering as if she was chilled through to her very bones and there was a sickening sense of hopelessness in her heart that offered no glimmer of relief.

'You know I wouldn't—I wouldn't have done this deliberately,' she whispered huskily. 'You can't believe that, Neil!'

'I have to believe what I see,' Neil rasped sharply. 'Nicky's gone, and that's proof enough that I was right to suspect something like this would happen. Michael Browlett gave enough warning when he turned up here that day you saw him. He's probably been around ever since waiting for his chance—a chance you presented to him on a plate this afternoon!'

'But——' Rachel bit her lip in anguish. 'If he has Nicky—how can he hope to keep him? The courts wouldn't let him have custody after all these years, surely they wouldn't, Neil!'

Neil's stern, rock-like features cracked briefly into a travesty of a smile as he looked down at her. 'Oh, he doesn't want Nicky,' he told her harshly. 'He just hopes to persuade me to pay for the privilege of keeping him. It isn't kidnapping, of course, he is Nicky's father, so they wouldn't call it that, but he knows that I'd sign over Nicky's inheritance, every last halfpenny of it, to have him back and to avoid putting Nicky through the agony of a court case over who has custody of him!' He looked as if he was about to say more, but after a second he made a short, sharp sound that dismissed her as a complete fool and strode across the hall to the telephone.

Rachel did nothing while he gave the basic story to the police over the telephone, and Lars did not even put a hand on her in an attempt to console her. It was not the moment for Lars to offer consolation, not with Neil's tall, vengeful figure only a few feet away, and anyway Rachel was inconsolable.

It was her fault, she could not deny that, even though Lars must inevitably share some of the blame; she had been entrusted with the care of Nicky and she had allowed herself to become so involved with Lars that she had lost sight and sound of Nicky completely. It was something that Neil prophesied could happen and now it had.

Neil put down the telephone and stood for a few seconds, quite still, his hands gripping the edge of the table and Rachel could see that his knuckles were white-boned in the strong brown fingers. Then he turned and faced them again, his eyes still cold, but darkened with the realisation that Nicky really was gone, and Rachel's heart yearned to comfort him.

'Neil——' She ventured a step towards him, but stopped short when he looked at her.

'Where were you when he—disappeared?' he asked in a cold flat voice, and Rachel instinctively glanced at Lars before she answered.

'Out there, in the front garden,' she said huskily, and anxiously ran her tongue over her dry lips. 'We were sitting on the low wall by the steps to the front door and Nicky was running around in and out of the shrubbery. We—we were talking and——'

'Talking!' His scorn hurt much more than he could ever know and Rachel flinched from it, but she held his gaze determinedly.

'We were talking,' she repeated in a small flat voice, 'and we didn't notice that Nicky—that we couldn't hear him any longer. Those engine noises he likes making when he's playing,' she explained when he looked briefly puzzled. 'It was when I went to call him to come in that——' She bit her lip hastily rather than let the tears cause a sob in her voice as they threatened to, but Neil's eyes were harshly unforgiving as he looked down at her.

'When you eventually remembered that you were responsible for him,' he said, and Rachel put a hand to her mouth, her eyes dark with anguish.

'It was as much my fault as Rachel's,' Lars intervened, and his voice shook with emotion.

Neil looked at him with narrowed eyes for a moment. 'I know that quite well,' he told him coldly, 'but neither of you could be trusted when it came to the point, could you? I thought Rachel was safe to leave in charge when you were around, I had her assurance on that and I believed her—it seems I was wrong after all!'

'Neil, for God's sake!' Lars curled his hands into tight hard fists and for a moment it looked as if he might strike out so that Rachel caught her breath and prayed that they would not take the quarrel any further. Lars drew in a deep audible breath and shook his head. 'Don't punish Rachel any more, Neil,' he said more quietly, 'she didn't let Nicky go deliberately, your own sense must tell you that!'

'Punish her?' Neil's blue eyes looked at Rachel for a moment, so cold and blank that she shivered under their scrutiny, her heart drumming hopelessly at her ribs. It was obvious that he had no idea how much he could hurt her, but Lars had seen and tried to help. 'What have I done to punish her?' Neil asked.

'Can't you see?' Lars asked. 'The fault was as much mine as Rachel's, and you can't go on——' He shrugged, his eyes on Rachel and so filled with compassion that she could not bear it.

She shook her head slowly, looking at Lars with her huge grey eyes dark with hurt. 'Don't, Lars,' she whispered. 'I—it doesn't matter.' She looked up at Neil, seeking some glimmer of compassion, but found none, only that cold blankness that refused to feel anything but the loss of Nicky. Then turning away hastily before she broke down and cried, she walked across the hall to the stairs—nothing anyone said now would make any difference.

The police had been polite and kind, and Rachel had gone through the motions of telling them what Nicky had been wearing, where and when she had last seen him and how long she and Lars had been before they noticed he was missing. It was an ordeal she suffered in a kind of trance, for she still found it hard to believe that Nicky could really be gone.

Lars too had talked to them, given them much the same information she had herself, and all the time Neil had sat and listened, saying nothing, his ice blue eyes watching them, impatient when they answered vaguely and never once giving Rachel the glimpse of warmth and understanding she sought so anxiously from him.

Mrs. Handley came in when the police had gone at last and asked if they wanted dinner at the usual time. Her eyes, Rachel noticed, were swollen with crying and she looked at Rachel only once and with such reproach that Rachel was close to tears again herself.

She instinctively shook her head at the idea of sitting down to a meal, but both Neil and Lars presumably found some kind of comfort in following the customary routine, so she was obliged to join them, a small silent figure with Nicky's empty chair beside her to remind her.

Once or twice Lars had looked across at her, but she had refused to meet his eyes, and the two men had gone over the last few minutes before Nicky's disappearance again and again until she could have screamed. 'He can't hope to get him out of the country with him,' Lars said, trying to sound more confident than he was, and for the first time Rachel realised the full possibilities of what had happened.

'He won't try to get him out of the country,' Neil argued in that same cold, flat voice he had used all along. 'Not until he's issued the ultimatum—told me what price I have to pay for getting Nicky back.'

Lars had smoked incessantly ever since Neil came back and he lit another cigarette now, his long hands not quite steady when he applied the flame to its tip. 'The money!' he said bitterly. 'It all boils down to Lynn's money, doesn't it? If only Nicky hadn't been willed all that money this would never have happened, there would have been no chance of it happening!'

Neil's blue eyes narrowed sharply and he too took another cigarette and lit it—both men, it was obvious, were far more nervously tense than their outward appearances first suggested. 'Who else could you expect Lynn to leave her money to?' he asked harshly. 'You surely didn't expect her to leave it to Browlett, did you?'

'No, of course not!' Lars shook his head. Resting his elbows on the table, he clasped his long hands together and frowned. 'The question is whether Michael Browlett will claim she was—well, not quite in her right mind when she made the will,' he suggested, and Neil again looked at him in sharp disagreement.

'Because of what happened last year?' he demanded in a voice that sent chills down Rachel's spine as she listened to it. Somehow she felt she should say something, break in and remind them that she was there, for they seemed to have forgotten her existence for the moment. They were like two antagonists in a ring, circling each other, finding each other's vulnerable spots, waiting to strike, and Rachel shivered at the prospect. 'You know better than anyone why that happened,' Neil said flatly, and Lars' good-looking face flushed as he ground out the barely touched cigarette with a fierceness that betrayed his anger.

'You'll never let me forget that, will you?' he asked in a voice little more than a whisper. He sat with his empty hands on the table in front of him for a long moment, then, as if he could stand their inactivity no longer, he reached for another cigarette and lit it. 'I can't believe that Lynn—did what she did because of a—lighthearted love affair,' he said. 'I did nothing to suggest it was anything else but lighthearted, and——'

'It wasn't lighthearted to Lynn!' Neil argued harshly, and despite her reluctance to be a witness to what must surely be a very private argument, Rachel found herself undeniably involved. Whatever had happened to Lynn Browlett a year ago, she was about to find out, and her heart was thudding so hard at her breast that she held her breath as she waited for Neil to go on. 'She loved you,' Neil said, 'and you didn't even realise it!'

'How could I?' Lars' voice had the sound of despair and, despite the fact that he appeared to be emerging as some kind of heartless philanderer, Rachel felt sorry for him. 'How could I know she meant to throw herself off the cliffs the minute I told her it was over? How could I know she'd try and take Nicky with her?'

Rachel felt cold and still suddenly, and the haunting shade of Lynn Browlett seemed stronger than ever it had as the three of them sat there round the table. Anger, resentment and her own cold realisation mingled in an atmosphere that hung over them like a tangible threat.

The truth about Lynn had proved to be far more awful than Rachel could ever have imagined, and for a few chilling moments she actually wondered if she could be having a nightmare and that none of it was true. She could, with little effort, visualise that pretty, petulant creature in the photograph being driven by despair to attempt her own life, but to try and take Nicky with her—

It was no wonder that Nicky was afraid of the sea and that Neil had forbidden her to take him anywhere near it; the wonder was that he was so well adjusted after all he had been through, and she felt her heart contract at the mere thought of him being with a man who, although he was his father, was in reality a stranger interested only in how much he was worth to him.

It was some time before Neil replied to Lars' anguished question, and Rachel found herself waiting as anxiously as Lars did. A spiral of blue smoke hid Neil's strong, rugged features and his eyes had the darkness of despair as he gazed down at his empty plate, his hands clasped in front of his face. There was an air of dejection about him that Rachel found hard to bear, and she longed to offer consolation—but how could she when she was the indirect cause of his misery?

Then he shook his head slowly, as if he was very tired. 'How could you know?' he echoed quietly.

'You never really knew Lynn at all, did you, Lars?' He looked up at last and straight at Lars, studying the good-looking face almost as if he was seeing it for the first time. 'But you keep coming back,' he said, and his voice implied a question, so that Lars looked at him curiously.

'You know why,' he told him. 'I care for Nicky as much as you do, Neil, I've never denied that.'

'But you wouldn't have married Lynn and given him a proper family and a home,' Neil said quietly. 'You *do* love him, I know that, that's why I've never suggested that you stay away from Seaways, and because I felt that somewhere inside you, you really did feel more for Lynn than a—a light-hearted affection. Lately, however——'

For the first time his eyes came to rest on Rachel and she shivered when she saw from their expression that he really had forgotten she was there. Lars too looked across at her as if he only now realised that he was not alone with his cousin, and his eyes took in the paleness of her face and the soft, hurt look about her mouth as she looked at Neil.

'I don't really think you have any more perception than I had with Lynn,' he told Neil, and Rachel saw the swift frown that drew Neil's fair brows together.

Lars, more perceptive where her feelings were concerned, had recognised her hurt and the reason for it before she had done so herself. It was only now when she looked at Neil and felt a great surge of pity and longing for him that she knew how much she loved him, and the realisation was, in the circumstances, almost unbearable.

She pushed back her chair and got to her feet in one swift nervous movement, avoiding Lars' expressive blue eyes that watched her with a kind of curious pity. Her main anxiety at the moment was to escape from the room before Neil too realised what she had only now learned about herself, and she did not stop to make formal excuses, but simply murmured a few almost inaudible words and hurried out of the room.

She could not leave Seaways until she knew Nicky was safely back with Neil, but as soon as she knew that there was no alternative for her but to go. To suppose he could feel anything but scorn for her after what had happened would be hopelessly optimistic, and she could not bear to stay, even if he allowed her to, knowing he despised her.

CHAPTER TEN

THE night had seemed endless to Rachel and she had lain in the darkness, her brain as well as her body refusing the sleep she ached for. Even the moon denied her the comfort of its light; hidden by clouds, it left her room as black as pitch while she lay and listened to the dreary rattle of rain on her window.

Even when the first chill light began to creep across the grey winter sky it found her still awake, haunted by things she had no power to change now. Neil's face was before her every time she closed her eyes—cold, angry and unrelenting. His harsh words still pricked her conscience.

Neither could she forget Nicky, alone somewhere, probably crying because there was nothing familiar and he could not understand why Neil had not come to take him home by now. The stranger who was his father, he had disliked on sight, and she remembered how he had come running back to her that day in the grounds whe Michael Browlett had appeared so unexpectedly.

Nicky had trusted her to protect him from the unknown as Neil had trusted her, and her heart thudded in despair when she realised how she had failed them both. Hidden away somewhere Nicky would be confused and frightened, and heaven knew what tortures Neil was going through, thinking about him. Turning suddenly, she buried her face in the pillows, smothering the despairing cry that rose to her lips, her only relief in tears.

There seemed to be no sound in the house when she lifted her head again, although something, she thought, had roused her from the misery of half-consciousness. Beyond the uncurtained window the light was a little stronger, though still grey and chill and darkened by clouds that scudded before an east wind that would cut like a knife. Her eyes felt swollen and tired with weeping and she could find no comfort in the dishevelled bed that she had tossed and turned in all night long—it was as well to leave it as to lie there any longer.

Moving almost unconsciously, she bathed and dressed, not caring what time it was and whether or not it was too early for anyone else to be about. There was no one at Seaways she could face in her present state. She carefully avoided looking into Nicky's room as she usually did in the morning, for he would not be in there and she could not bear the sight of his small bed bereft of its occupant.

She went downstairs, dazed from lack of sleep, and it was only when she got down into the hall that she realised she had put on a topcoat over her indoor clothes. It seemed as if some instinct had prompted her to dress for going out, to take a walk as a means of avoiding the ordeal of breakfasting with Neil and Lars and also to inject some activity into her weary limbs. There was no one about when she opened the front door, and she closed it behind her, quite unaware that she was being observed from the doorway of the kitchen.

Rachel took the longer, road way to the sea, for even in her present fuddled state she could realise the impracticability of trying to walk across the heavy clay of ploughed fields after last night's rain, and her appearance drew more than one curious look from early rising farmworkers as she made her way along the narrow, winding lanes to the sea.

The day was scarcely begun yet, but already she foresaw little promise of anything but more unhappiness, and she impatiently brushed a hand across her eyes when the haze of tears briefly obscured her vision. She felt so helpless and yet there was little she could do personally about finding Nicky—the people with the experience and best qualified to search for him were already doing all they could.

Seeking some small consolation, she told herself that both Nicky and his father were good-looking enough to draw second glances, and if Nicky was as unhappy as she knew he would be his tears would almost certainly attract attention too. The prospect of him not being found did not bear thinking about, but at the moment her own misery occupied her almost as much as Nicky's did.

She must face the future without Neil, that much was certain, and even thinking about never seeing him again once she left Seaways brought the tears flooding into her eyes again. If only she could have realised sooner how much she loved him, then she could have acted very differently.

She could see now that Neil had offered her something very precious during those few weeks Lars had been away and she had been too blind to see it.

She shook her head, again using an impatient hand to brush away the tears, dismissing the what might have been as beyond recall—there was nothing to be done about it now. There was a slight break in the scudding clouds suddenly and for a moment she caught a glimpse of a pale ice blue sky above the grey—if only her own outlook offered as much hope she could have been happier.

Nearer the sea the wind took on an even harsher chill and she shivered as she looked across at the thick dark soil turned into neat furls by the plough. Overhead a cloud of screaming seagulls swept down, squabbling among themselves, their noise frightening off the quieter lapwings who also gleaned a harvest from the bare clods, the wind carrying their high plaintive cries to her above the chatter of the gulls.

Heaven knew why she had chosen to come this way, unless it was because Lynn Browlett was so recently in her thoughts, but somehow she felt that the grey turbulent mood of the winter sea would fit in with her own melancholy. The wind was much colder even than she had expected and she shivered as she made her way along the cliff top, her long hair whipping back from her face and her cheeks stinging with the salt-laden dampness.

Below was the narrow strip of beach where she had walked, and she shuddered when she remembered that icy drenching and how she had clung so desperately to the narrow ledge above the water until Neil came and rescued her. She had not realised then how much more painful it must have been for him than she suspected to pluck her from the same hungry tide that had killed his sister.

Poor Neil, he had had so much to face during the past few years, and now she had by her carelessness delivered him yet another blow. She had learned from Lars that Neil's father had died only a short time after Lynn ran off with Michael Browlett, and then, when her husband deserted her, Neil had given Lynn and her baby a home with him.

He had seen her through that only to have her enter into a romance with their cousin that was bound to end with someone getting hurt. And when Lynn took her dramatic way out it was Neil once again who picked up the pieces and made a home with him for Nicky. It was no wonder that he had judged her in that cold, hurt anger when she had lost him the one person in the world he really cared about.

Because she loved him she suddenly felt every hurt as if it was her own, and now that there was no one else about to see, she let the tears roll down her cheeks unchecked, but even that brought no relief. Neil would never trust her again, and she did not see how she was going to bear the hurt of leaving him.

She clenched her hands tightly in the pockets of her coat and looked down at the restless grey surface of the sea, shaking her head as the cold wind whipped her hair back and stung her cheeks like ice. At last she could identify with Lynn; she knew exactly how she had felt when she had come up here to the cliff top, in despair because she loved Lars too much to face life without him.

Those angry grey waters crashing against the cliff face offered an end to the agony of a life without Neil—to the bitter anguish that held her body stiff and cold against the icy wind.

Rachel was so cold that her limbs felt numb and immovable and she stirred at last, drawing a deep shuddering breath and brushing one hand across her cold cheeks where the tears had dried into her soft skin and left it stiff and dry. She had no watch with her, but she could see from the state of the tide below that she had been there for some time, just standing there on the cliff, staring down at the angry, grey cold sea and thinking about Neil.

Her feet were chill and ached with cold and her hands too, despite the comparative warmth of the coat pockets, were stiff and unresponsive when she tried to pull up her coat collar closer round her face. If anyone had missed her at Seaways it would be presumed she was still sleeping, and she almost wished she was. She would have given almost anything to arouse enough feeling in Neil to make him come out and look for her as he had done before.

Taking a last shuddering look at the sea crashing on to the rocks in white-foamed fury, she turned and made her way back along the cliff. The wind was now partly behind her, blowing her hair up and over her face as she walked, and she needed one hand to brush it away every few seconds so that she could see where she was walking.

It was when she cleared its long strands from her eyes that she suddenly realised that someone was coming towards her, braving the wind in the opposite direction, and for a moment her heart almost stood still when she recognised him.

There was no mistaking those long anxious strides that brought him closer with every second, or the thick blond hair blown into confusion as her own was, the features carved in golden granite above the collar of a sheepskin jacket that swung open as it almost always did. A big, awesome yet comforting figure that was coming straight for her, and her legs almost gave way beneath her as she stopped dead, her eyes wide and anxious in the pale oval of her face.

She tried to judge if it was anger that lent such urgency to his stride, but at a distance it was impossible to tell, and at the moment she would have welcomed even his anger as long as he was there. Trembling, she watched as he came closer and saw the drawn cold look on his face mellowed into a sudden warmth.

He said nothing at first, but she was snatched into his arms and held closely against that warm, powerful body, closing her eyes on the sheer ecstasy of it. His hands, strong and gentle, were soothing, comforting and unbelievably exciting as he slid them beneath her coat and the warm wings of his jacket enfolded her as they had done once before when they stood in that small bobbing boat below the cliffs.

He buried his face in the wind-tossed tangle of her dark hair and his voice spoke softly against her ear. 'He's back, Rachel!' and for a moment she even had to stop and remember that it was Nicky he referred to.

She raised her face at last, her eyes wide and doubtful, wanting to believe she had heard him aright but scarcely daring to. She licked her parched lips and they tasted dry and salty. 'Nicky?' she whispered. 'Nicky's back?'

Neil nodded and the look in his blue eyes was enough to convince her that it was true. 'They were found last night in a hotel in London,' he told her. 'The police brought him home this morning and he's already asleep.'

'Oh, thank God!' She closed her eyes and for a moment she seemed to sway, even in the firm closeness of his arms. The relief she felt left her feeling incredibly weak and suddenly nothing was impossible.

Neil drew her close again, burying his face in her hair, his voice muffled when he spoke again. 'And no sooner have I recovered from one shock than you give me another,' he said huskily. 'I wanted to tell you that they'd brought Nicky home, I couldn't wait for you to come down, and——' He laughed, and it was a short and oddly shaky sound as if he had been close to tears, 'Mrs. Handley said you weren't there!'

'Oh, Neil!'

He pressed his mouth to her cheek, that short, anxious laugh fluttering against her hair again as he hugged her close. 'You weren't there, Rachel—how could you *do* that to me?'

Rachel said nothing, but her fingers, stiff and cold as they were, conveyed her contrition as plainly as if she had spoken it. The softness of his sweater was warm on her palms and her fingers explored the suggestion of smooth skin beneath it, a warm sensual excitement running through her whole being as she stood enfolded in his arms.

'Mrs. Handley saw you leave the house,' he told her, still in that strangely muffled voice that suggested a panic only just abated, 'and I couldn't believe it at first—I thought you were still sleeping!'

'I didn't sleep,' She looked up at him, the dark rings of weariness evident about her grey eyes and he bent his head and gently kissed her lowered lids. 'I didn't hear Nicky come back either,' she said, frowning curiously. 'How could I not hear him, Neil, when he's in the next room?'

'Because he was afraid of being alone,' Neil told her softly. 'I put him into my bed and stayed with him until he went to sleep—I thought you were asleep too, but I would have woken you to tell you he was home. When Mrs. Handley said she'd seen you go out——'

'You knew where to find me!' Rachel guessed, but he shook his head and the arms around her held her even more tightly.

'She had misgivings, seeing you go out so early,'

he said huskily, 'and she went upstairs to see which way you went, but she hadn't the sense to tell me, to tell somebody that you'd taken the sea road—my God, I could have hit her!'

'Neil!'

She whispered his name, her face still pressing to the broad comfort of his chest, and Neil kissed the softness of her neck with infinite gentleness. 'I was so afraid,' he confessed in a whisper. 'I was so afraid of what I'd find, my love!'

My love! Rachel lifted her head again and her eyes were bright and warm between the fringe of dark lashes that still looked spiky with tears. 'I didn't think,' she confessed. 'I suppose—I suppose I thought you wouldn't care one way or the other, after what I did.'

Neil looked down at her, his blue eyes never less icy-looking than now, and there was a half smile on his wide mouth that gave Rachel the urgent desire to be kissed. Instead he studied her for a long moment, his eyes searching every feature of her flushed face, lingering on her mouth in the way that sent a shiver through her.

'I could more easily have made allowances for what happened,' Neil said quietly, 'if only you hadn't been with Lars. That hurt more than you'll ever know!'

Rachel shook her head and her fingers stroked the soft wool of his sweater, lingering on the spot where the steady beat of his heart pulsed with life. 'You just wouldn't believe I wasn't in love with Lars,' she reproached him, and Neil kissed her mouth lightly before he answered.

'I didn't know what to believe, Rachel,' he said gently. 'I'd seen it all before and——' He stopped and shook his head. 'I was so unsure, I know how— potent Lars can be, and you admitted that you found him attractive.'

Rachel traced a pattern on the thick wool sweater with a fingertip and lowered lids hid her eyes from him. 'He—he wanted me to go to Sweden with him,' she said, and raised her eyes suddenly to look at him, her eyes bright with a hint of challenge. '*He* knew why I wouldn't go!' she told him in a small breathless voice, and Neil bent his head swiftly, his mouth hard and urgent on hers, making her catch her breath and curl her hands against the broad warmth of his chest.

Elatedly certain at last, Rachel yielded to the demands he made on her, every nerve of her body responding to the strong, gentle persuasiveness of his. The wind could have been as cold as ice, she had never felt more glowingly warm, and her heart beat wildly, uncontrollably in response to new sensations that aroused desires in her she had never thought herself capable of.

Holding her close, Neil looked down at her, saying nothing for a few seconds, his eyes once again searching her face, as if he would never tire of looking at it. 'I could only think of you last night,' he told her in a deep, soft voice that did incredible things to her emotions.

'Your pale little face and big eyes—I must have been blind and insane to treat you the way I did and to let you go like that. I should have comforted you and instead I was angry, angry and hurt because I knew you'd been with Lars when Nicky was taken. I didn't expect to sleep last night, but it wasn't Nicky who haunted me, it was you, and this morning when you were gone——' He shuddered and the force of it touched her own body, making her tremble. 'Can you ever forgive me, Rachel?'

'Forgive you?' She reached up and touched his strong, rugged jaw gently with a fingertip. 'I love you, and the fact that you're here now makes anything else unimportant.' She lifted her face and kissed him lightly on his mouth. 'I hurt you,' she said softly, 'but I didn't mean to. I'd never hurt you the way your sister did, Neil, you must know that.'

'I know that now,' he echoed. 'You'd never be as foolish as poor little Lynn.'

It was easier now to mention Lynn, now that Neil had spoken about her, and she looked up at him for a moment, her eyes seeking some likeness to the photograph she had seen on Lars' bedside table. 'I—I saw a picture of her in Lars' room when the door was open one day,' she told him. 'She—you weren't very much alike, were you?'

He said nothing for a moment, then he turned her in his arms and hugged her close to him as they started to walk back along the cliff. 'Lynn was only my half-sister,' he said, and his voice was quiet and steady, confiding at last the way she had always hoped he would.

'She was a silly, pretty little creature, but I loved her, perhaps because of what she was rather than in spite of it. She was only seventeen when she ran off with Browlett and I suppose we could have stopped them, but——' He spread one large hand in a gesture of helplessness. 'My father doted on her and it was always difficult to be angry with Lynn. Nicky's very much like her.'

'I thought so,' Rachel agreed quietly, and Neil looked down at her for a moment with a curiously unfathomable look in his eyes.

'You know about her and Lars?' he asked, and it was plain that even now he did not find it easy to talk about it.

Rachel nodded, hugging herself more close to him as she spoke, anxious to let him know she understood. 'I know,' she said. 'In part you told me yourself, when you and Neil were arguing in the stable one day and you mentioned her again the day you and Lars——'

'When I warned him not to hurt you the way he had Lynn!' he said shortly, and for a moment there was a trace of that cold anger in his voice. 'If he had, I'd never have forgiven him!'

'And yet you forgave him for Lynn,' she suggested gently, and Neil looked at her for a moment steadily, his blue eyes dark with something that touched a response in every nerve of Rachel's body.

'I forgave him for Lynn,' he agreed quietly, 'but what happened was, in part, Lynn's own fault. I warned her, but she wouldn't listen, any more than she would when my father warned her about Michael Browlett. Lynn was young and very easily swept into an affair, but she wasn't as—as vulner-

186

able as you are, my darling.'

'Neil!' She turned and faced him again, drawn into the warmth of his arms again, enfolded in the strong, masculine force that shivered through her own body like fire and ice.

His blue eyes held a glistening warmth she had never seen there before and she reached up her arms and circled his neck, her fingers gently stroking the thick blond hair that curled above the collar of his jacket. 'I love you,' he said softly. 'If I *had* lost you to Lars or to——' He glanced briefly at the cold grey tide below the cliff and shook his head. 'I couldn't have faced it, Rachel, even with Nicky back I couldn't have faced losing you!'

Rachel leaned back against his arms, her grey eyes more bright than ever when she looked at him. That dear, familiar face with its deceptively stern mouth and ice blue eyes was something she would never grow tired of looking at, and she smiled suddenly. 'I don't think I could have gone,' she confessed. 'Somehow or other I'd have found a way to stay near you—and you still need someone to take care of Nicky.'

'From now on I'll take care of both of you,' Neil told her, and pulled her close into his arms again, his mouth seeking hers just as that little patch of blue winter sky appeared from behind the clouds again.

romance is beautiful!

**· and Harlequin Reader Service
is your passport to the
Heart of Harlequin**

Harlequin is the world's leading publisher of romantic fiction novels. If you enjoy the mystery and adventure of romance, then you will want to keep up to date on all of our new monthly releases—eight brand new Romances and four Harlequin Presents.

If you are interested in catching up on exciting and valuable back issues, Harlequin Reader Service offers **a** wide choice of best-selling novels reissued for your reading enjoyment.

If you want a truly jumbo read and a money-saving value, the Harlequin Omnibus offers three intriguing novels under one cover by one of your favorite authors.

To find out more about Harlequin, the following information will be your passport to the Heart of Harlequin.

collection editions

**Rare Vintage Romance
From Harlequin**

The Harlequin Collection editions have been chosen
from our 400 through 899 series, and comprise some of
our earliest and most sought-after titles. Most of the
novels in this series have not been available since the
original publication and are available now in beautifully
redesigned covers.

When complete, these unique books will comprise the
finest collection of vintage romance novels available.
You will treasure reading and owning this delightful
library of beautiful love stories for many years to come.

For further information, turn to the back of this book and
return the INFORMATION PLEASE coupon.

the omnibus

A Great Idea! Three great romances by the same author, in one deluxe paperback volume.

A Great Value! Almost 600 pages of pure entertainment for only $1.95 per volume.

Essie Summers

Bride in Flight (#933)
...begins on the eve of Kirsty's wedding with the strange phone call that changed her life. Blindly, instinctively Kirsty ran — but even New Zealand wasn't far enough to avoid the complications that followed!

Postscript to Yesterday (#1119)
...Nicola was dirty, exasperated and a little bit frightened. She was in no shape after her amateur mechanics on the car to meet any man, let alone Forbes Westerfield. He was the man who had told her not to come.

Meet on My Ground (#1326)
...is the story of two people in love, separated by pride. Alastair Campbell had money and position — Sarah Macdonald was a girl with pride. But pride was no comfort to her at all after she'd let Alastair go!

Jean S. MacLeod

The Wolf of Heimra (#990)
...Fenella knew that in spite of her love for the island, she had no claim on Heimra yet — until an heir was born. These MacKails were so sure of themselves; they expected everything to come their way.

Summer Island (#1314)
...Cathie's return to Loch Arden was traumatic. She knew she was clinging to the past, refusing to let it go. But change was something you thought of happening in other places — never in your own beloved glen.

Slave of the Wind (#1339)
...Lesley's pleasure on homecoming and meeting the handsome stranger quickly changed to dismay when she discovered that he was Maxwell Croy — the man whose family once owned her home. And Maxwell was determined to get it back again.

Susan Barrie

Marry a Stranger (#1034)
...if she lived to be a hundred, Stacey knew she'd never be more violently in love than she was at this moment. But Edouard had told her bluntly that he would never fall in love with her!

Rose in the Bud (#1168)
...One thing Cathleen learned in Venice: it was highly important to be cautious when a man was a stranger and inhabited a world unfamiliar to her. The more charm he possessed, the more wary she should be!

The Marriage Wheel (#1311)
...Admittedly the job was unusual — lady chauffeur to Humphrey Lestrode; and admittedly Humphrey was high-handed and arrogant. Nevertheless Frederica was enjoying her work at Farthing Hall. Then along came her mother and beautiful sister, Rosaleen, to upset everything.

Violet Winspear

Beloved Tyrant (#1032)
...Monterey was a beautiful place to recuperate. Lyn's job was interesting. Everything, in fact, would have been perfect, Lyn Gilmore thought, if it hadn't been for the hateful Rick Corderas. He made her feel alive again!

Court of the Veils (#1267)
...In the lush plantation on the edge of the Sahara, Roslyn Brant tried very hard to remember her fiancé and her past. But the bitter, disillusioned Duane Hunter refused to believe that she ever was engaged to his cousin, Armand.

Palace of the Peacocks (#1318)
...Suddenly the island, this exotic place that so recently had given her sanctuary, seemed an unlucky place rather than a magical one. She must get away from the cold palace and its ghost — and especially from Ryk van Helden.

Isobel Chace

The Saffron Sky (#1250)
...set in a tiny village skirting the exotic Bangkok, Siam, the small, nervous Myfanwy Jones realizes her most cherished dream, adventure and romance in a far-off land. Two handsome men determine to marry her, but both have the same mysterious reason....

A Handful of Silver (#1306)
...in exciting Rio de Janeiro, city of endless beaches and skyscraper hotels, a battle of wits is waged between Madelaine Delahaye, Pilar Fernandez, the jealous fiancée of her childhood friend, and her handsome, treacherous cousin — Luis da Maestro....

The Damask Rose (#1334)
...Vicki Tremaine flies to the heady atmosphere of Damascus to meet Adam Templeton, fiancé of the rebellious Miriam. But alas, as time passes, Vicki only becomes more attracted to this young Englishman with the steel-like personality....

information please

**All the Exciting News from
Under the Harlequin Sun**

It costs you nothing to receive our news bulletins and intriguing brochures. From our brand new releases to our money-saving 3-in-1 omnibus and valuable best-selling back titles, our information package is sure to be a hit. Don't miss out on any of the exciting details. Send for your Harlequin INFORMATION PLEASE package today.